CW00555317

THE MAN WHO MARRIED HIMSELF AND OTHER STORIES

by Charlie Fish

Dedicated to Emma

The Man Who Married Himself and Other Stories
is published by Charlie Fish, 121 Leigham Vale, London SW2
3JH, United Kingdom

Cover design by Dave Aldhouse.
Illustrations by Yvette Gilbert.
Typesetting by Samia Asif.

ISBN 978-0-9926939-2-3

This is a Free Cultural Work by Charlie Fish, 2021.

This work is licensed under the Creative Commons Attribution
4.0 International License. To view a copy of this license, visit
http://creativecommons.org/licenses/by/4.0/

Website: www.fictionontheweb.co.uk

Selected reviews from East of the Web.

Baggio's Story

- I think this story changed me a little bit. Maybe a lot.

- Solid! Fantastic! Dramatic! True!

- Charlie Fish, you have done it again. Thank you. Need to reread this story and I will. Many times. I expect to get more and more out of it every time I do.

- This is probably THE BEST short story I've ever read in my life. It really taught me a valuable lesson on the materialistic things in this world.

- i kinda didn't read . . . cuz it was tOO long . . :P LOL :D

Cora

- Oh My God! I love your story. I'm a writer myself and it takes a lot to impress me. I'm a picky reader, but your story drew me in and held me tight!

- This is by far one of the best short stories I have ever read. From the beginning to the end, I was on the edge of my seat. Great work Charlie. I can't wait to see what's next.

- Fantastic job. It was mental coffee. It held my attention and slowly pulled me in as the story progressed. I appreciate the way it flirted with my imagination.

- This is an amazing story. I've recently been using Fish's stories as part of my unit plans for high schoolers . . . Great author! This guy can really put a lot into just a few pages.

- i hate this story..................... if you don't no how to write don't write............

The Man Who Married Himself

- This Charlie Fish guy needs to be watched he is seriously talented.

- Hilarious. A real breath of fresh air. There is a lightness, a flow to Charlie's writing that seems to create intelligent humor out of subject matter that commonly would be deemed very over-the-top. A great chop to the groin. I think I'll share this one around a bit.

- I found myself chuckling openly all the way through it at some priceless lines . . . Funny in the extreme, I enjoyed it immensely.

- I loved this story! I had to stop myself from laughing several times. I would recommend this story and I will use it with my high school students I teach.

- well ya u see this story wasnt all that good and trust me i know good storie i read alot of books cuz its are assignment im locked up in the salt lake vally D.T well thats me opinion

Death by Scrabble

- I love this story and so do my students. I teach it in my high school classes every year, and every year someone uses it on their state exam.

- Splendid!!! So outrageous it kept me laughing. One of my favorite stories. This author's writing style reminds me of Sydney Sheldon's – get-to-the-point-and-keep-moving, which keeps the reader's interest.

- I really loved this story. It had a feel of O. Henry or better still, Alfred Hitchcock about it.

- Excellent story. Reminded me very much of my wife and I. Therefore horribly frightening.

- This was the GREATEST thing I have ever seen! My heart almost stopped beating with the suspense! Charlie Fish is an absolute GOD, I want to marry him. I WANT MORE!!!!!!!

TABLE OF CONTENTS

DEATH BY SCRABBLE

I find myself thinking – the letters will tell me what to do.

It's a hot day and I hate my wife.

We're playing Scrabble. That's how bad it is. I'm forty-two years old, it's a blistering hot Sunday afternoon and all I can think of to do with my life is play Scrabble.

I should be out, doing exercise, spending money, meeting people. I don't think I've spoken to anyone except my wife since Thursday morning. On Thursday morning I spoke to the milkman.

My letters are crap.

I play, appropriately, BEGIN. With the N on the little pink star. Twenty-two points.

I watch my wife's smug expression as she rearranges her letters. Clack, clack, clack. I hate her. If she wasn't around, I'd be doing something interesting right now. I'd be climbing Mount Kilimanjaro. I'd be starring in the latest Hollywood blockbuster. I'd be sailing the Vendée Globe on a sixty-foot clipper called New Horizons – I don't know, but I'd be doing something.

She plays JINXED, with the J on a double-letter score. Thirty points. She's beating me already. Maybe I should kill her.

If only I had a D, then I could play MURDER. That would be a sign. That would be permission.

I start chewing on my U. It's a bad habit, I know. All the letters are frayed. I play WARMER for twenty-two more points, mainly so I can keep chewing on my U.

As I'm picking new letters from the bag, I find myself thinking – the letters will tell me what to do. If they spell out KILL, or STAB, or her name, or anything, I'll do it right now. I'll finish her off.

My rack spells MIHZPA. Plus the U in my mouth. Damn.

The heat of the sun is pushing at me through the window. I can hear buzzing insects outside. I hope they're not bees. My cousin Harold swallowed a bee when he was nine, his throat swelled up and he died. I hope that if they are bees, they fly into my wife's throat.

She plays SWEATIER, using all her letters. Twenty-four points plus a fifty-point bonus. If it wasn't too hot to move I would strangle her right now.

I am getting sweatier. It needs to rain, to clear the air. As soon as that thought crosses my mind, I find a good word. HUMID on a double-word score, using the D of JINXED. The U makes a little splash of saliva when I put it down. Another twenty-two points. I hope she has lousy letters.

She tells me she has lousy letters. For some reason, I hate her more.

She plays FAN, with the F on a double letter, and gets up to fill the kettle and turn on the air conditioning.

It's the hottest day for ten years and my wife is turning on the kettle. This is why I hate my wife. I play ZAPS, with the Z doubled, and she gets a static shock off the air-conditioning unit. I find this remarkably satisfying.

She sits back down with a heavy sigh and starts fiddling with her letters again. Clack clack. Clack clack. I feel a terrible rage build up inside me. Some inner poison slowly spreading through my limbs, and when it gets to my fingertips I'm going to jump out of my chair, spilling the Scrabble tiles over the floor, and I'm going to start hitting her again and again and again.

The rage gets to my fingertips – and passes. My heart is beating. I'm sweating. I think my face actually twitches. Then I sigh, deeply, and sit back into my chair. The kettle starts whistling. As the whistle builds it makes me feel hotter.

She plays READY on a double word for eighteen points, then goes to pour herself a mug of tea. No I do not want one.

I steal a blank tile from the letter bag when she's not looking, and throw back a V from my rack. She gives me a suspicious look. She sits down with her tea, making a cup ring on the table, as I play an eight-letter word: CHEATING, using the A of READY. Sixty-four points, including the fifty-point bonus, which means I'm beating her now.

She asks me if I cheated.

I really, really hate her.

She plays IGNORE on the triple word for twenty-one points. The score is 153 to her, 155 to me.

The steam rising from her cup of tea makes me feel hotter. I try to make murderous words with the letters on my rack. If only there was some way for me to get rid of her.

I spot a chance to use all my letters. EXPLODES, using the X of JINXED. Seventy-two points. That'll show her.

As I put the last letter down, there is a deafening bang and the air-conditioning unit fails.

My heart is racing, but not from the shock of the bang. I don't believe it – but it can't be a coincidence. The letters made it happen. I played the word EXPLODES, and it happened – the air-conditioning unit exploded. And before, I played the word CHEATING when I cheated. And ZAP when my wife got the electric shock. The words are coming true. The letters are choosing their future. The whole game is – JINXED.

My wife plays SIGN for ten points.

I have to test this.

I have to play something and see if it happens. Something unlikely, to prove that the letters are making it happen. My rack is ABQYFWE. That doesn't leave me with a lot of options. I start frantically chewing on the B.

I play FLY, using the L of EXPLODES. I sit back and close my eyes, waiting for the sensation of rising up from my chair. Waiting to fly.

Stupid. I open my eyes, and there's a fly. Buzzing around above the Scrabble board, surfing the thermals from the tepid cup of tea. That proves nothing. The fly could have been there anyway.

I need to play something unambiguous. Something that cannot be misinterpreted. Something absolute and final.

My wife plays CAUTION, using a blank tile for the N. Eighteen points.

My rack is AQWEUK, plus the B in my mouth. I'm awed by the power of the letters, and frustrated that I can't wield it. Maybe I should cheat again, and pick out the letters I need to spell SLASH or SLAY.

Then it hits me. The perfect word. A powerful, dangerous, terrible word.

I play QUAKE for nineteen points.

I wonder if the strength of the quake will be proportionate to how many points it scored. I can feel the trembling energy of potential in my veins. I am commanding fate. I am manipulating destiny.

My wife plays DEATH for thirty-four points, just as the room starts to shake.

I gasp with surprise and vindication – and the B that I was chewing on gets lodged in my throat. I try to cough. My throat swells. I draw blood clawing at my neck. The earthquake builds to a climax.

I fall to the floor. My wife just sits there, watching.

First published at www.eastoftheweb.com

I'm amazed and flattered that this story has resonated with so many people around the world. It has been published in school textbooks. It has been translated into several languages. It has been adapted into a short film dozens of times – see for yourself by searching for Death by Scrabble on YouTube.

I wrote the first draft in an afternoon of fevered inspiration, at my mother's house in 2005. With a Scrabble board at hand, of course. It was important to me – I don't know why – that the in-story game was realistic. I wrote the story with a view to being read aloud, so I could enter it into a BBC Radio 4 short story competition – it didn't place.

I used to play Scrabble with my grandmother, for whom English was her third or fourth language (after German, Greek and French), and she routinely wiped the floor with me. It was a real rite of passage into adulthood when I started beating her more often than she beat me.

Later, I rediscovered Scrabble (or rather recontextualised it) by playing high-stakes Scrabble with my girlfriend at university. We had a list of dares – if our combined score at the end of the game was low the loser would have to do an easy dare like doing everyone's washing up; but if our combined score was high the loser had to do something severe. That's how I ended up with my Scrabble-tiles tattoo. Decades later we're married with two kids, so that worked.

KILLING MILDRED

Mildred was the reason I stayed at the Manor. She was also the reason I left.

I paid my way through university by doing evening shifts as a care assistant at Brookbourne Manor. Before that I did bar work, but I hated it, so I traded the fusty smell of sweat and beer for the sting of ammonia and carbolic acid.

The Manor had sixteen residents, most of the time. My job was to clear away their supper and do the dishes, then help put them all to bed. That rarely took less than five hours between the two of us.

When I say the two of us, I mean Dani and me. She'd done this job for ten years. She was thirty-something, a mother of two, and a real prankster. She teased me no end. I hated it sometimes, but her stories kept the residents entertained.

On my first night she showed me Mrs Thwaite's bedtime routine. Mrs Thwaite was frail as a breadstick; we had to help her undress and toilet. (There's a verb I've never used outside of that job – to toilet.) After Mrs Thwaite was done toileting she called us back in and we pulled her to her feet.

"I'll back off now and talk you through it," Dani said, leaving Mrs Thwaite, half-naked, propped up against the basin. "First, wipe her bum."

Eager to make a good impression, I didn't hesitate. I unrolled three sheets, folded them around my fingers as a barrier, and tenderly applied them to Mrs Thwaite, who winced and sucked her teeth.

"OK, now you look at her poo, see if there's any blood in it," said Dani.

I looked in the toilet bowl. Just one pebble, black like a raisin.

"And you smell it, see if it's normal, like."

I took a deep lungful.

"OK, flush, and put just a touch of talc on her pussy."

I looked at Dani, ready to admonish her for using such disrespectful language. Her expression was earnest. I looked at Mrs Thwaite, whose hollow face remained perfectly vacant, and my confidence dissolved. I tipped some talcum powder onto my hand and patted it on.

Mrs Thwaite's eyes flicked downwards, then returned to the mirror above the basin. Apart from that, she didn't move. Dani managed to keep a straight face for about three seconds before exploding into a mocking laugh. She told that story, about how she had made me pad Mrs Thwaite's pussy, for months afterwards. It was a year before I realised I wasn't supposed to smell the residents' poo.

So, yes, Dani was a practical joker. Her mood carried the whole place. When she was larking around and making fun of me, the residents complained less and things went more smoothly. We all quietly feared the times when Dani came in feeling low. She'd start talking about how her life was going nowhere and suddenly Dennis's liver would play up, Mildred would start vomiting, Floris would cry, Mr Anders would refuse to eat . . . I would gladly trade that for a dose of humiliation as the butt of a practical joke.

Even when the residents were in relatively good spirits they did a lot of complaining. Especially Mrs Cobbler. Every day after supper she hobbled into the lounge, clutching her Zimmer frame with knurled fists, and commandeered the remote control for *EastEnders*. God forbid anyone should want to watch something else, or – worse – be sitting in her chair. She once laid out Mr Davies for suggesting that they switch over to the horse-racing. He hit his head on the coffee table and bled all over the Axminster. I had to bind his head with a tea towel until the ambulance came and we never saw him again.

But even when Mrs Cobbler got her way, as she always did, she complained. The volume was too low, or too high, or there was a glare on the screen, or Mildred was making too much noise, or Dennis was in the way. It was her hobby, I suppose. There was nothing else to do.

There really was nothing for them to do. Very few of them ever left the Manor. Visitors were rare. They were like mice in a maze, lost in little circles. Dani and I tried to come up with new ways to entertain them. We arranged a bingo night, and a poker night. We rented movies. I always promised Mrs Farrier a game of Scrabble, but never got round to it. We even took Dennis out to the local pub once – off duty, of course. He got so drunk he tried to chat up the cigarette machine and we had to carry him back to the Manor while he recited "Shtop all the clocksh" to the evening air.

Only one resident always had a smile on her face. Mildred Merrihap. My favourite.

When I hated my job most, I spoke to Mildred and she would give me courage. When Mrs Thwaite had a rectal prolapse from straining too hard on the toilet and I had nightmares for days about shitting out my lungs, or when I was shaving around Mr Anders' stoma so the colostomy bag would stick, and I nicked a bit of skin, and there was blood and shit everywhere and it smelled like dead birds – Mildred Merrihap got me through.

Mildred suffered from the most severe case of senile dementia I've ever witnessed. She wandered around the Manor gibbering and jabbering to herself, drooling fetid saliva from her brown-toothed mouth. But she was always smiling, always seemed to be enjoying herself.

"How are you today, Mildred?" I would ask her.

"And he said he wanted to grow rhododendrons!" she'd respond and laugh as if it was the punchline to a joke she'd been building up to for twenty minutes.

"Who said they wanted to grow rhododendrons?" I'd ask, fascinated by her parallel world.

"Yes, yes, and how are you doing at school?" she'd say, beaming.

"Well, university's hard work at the moment, as it happens," I'd say, speaking slowly in case she understood. "I have exams coming up next week and I don't feel ready. I'm not even sure I've chosen the right degree."

"Rupert called, did he? He's such a kind man." She'd shake her head in happy reminiscence. "He bought me flowers once, you know."

"Who's Rupert?" I'd ask, and so the conversation would spiral onwards. Her smile was broken and ugly and smelled of old grass, but she was so carefree it never failed to make me feel better.

I confess, I gave Mildred preferential treatment. When it came to the bedtime rounds, I rushed through Cobbler, Thwaite, Farrier, the Anderses, Dennis, Floris, whoever else, and saved Mildred for last. I spent twice as long cleaning her up and changing her, chatting non-stop.

My life was moving fast back then. The beats that marked time passing – that marked my growing up – were vivid. Graduating from school, leaving my parents' home, starting university, losing my virginity, my first this, my first that. It felt like a different world when I came to the Manor. A slower world, not somewhere I really belonged. Here the beats were faint, a fading pulse.

Mildred was the only person I could talk to about how I felt. Not just in the Manor, but anywhere. I told her things I didn't even tell my best friends. I told her how it might have been my fault when I crashed my flatmate's car. I told her how anxious I was about going back to live with my parents for the summer. I told her when Mr Anders soiled his bed and I couldn't bear to deal with it so I pretended I hadn't noticed and left it for Dani.

And she always responded with meaningless half sentences and semi-articulated recollections of unknown friends. She kept all my secrets and fears locked up inside her where no one could get at them.

Mildred was the reason I stayed at the Manor. She was also the reason I left.

At the beginning of my final year at university, Mildred fell ill. She started going straight back to bed as soon as the morning staff got her out, and then she stopped eating, and soon she had a temperature. She deteriorated quickly; one week I was joking with her about how awful it was to be ill, and the next week I was feeding her through a syringe.

My stomach tightened when her joyous smile was interrupted by moans from some uncommunicated pain. She stopped talking about chrysanthemums and Joe from down the road, and descended into feverish mumblings.

In the third week of her illness, Dani and I checked on Mildred in her room every half hour. We wedged her into the high-backed armchair with pillows, and wrapped her in quilts. She looked small and still, breathing fast like a mouse; and she was completely unresponsive. Dani even balanced a teacup on her head for me to find when I next checked up on her.

After I'd cleared away the teas and coffees and finished washing the dishes, I puréed a portion of chicken and veg for Mildred, funnelled it into the plastic syringe and went up to feed her.

Her eyes were closed and she was murmuring quietly. I knelt down and put my head next to hers. All of the creases on her forehead were knotted together at a point behind the bridge of her glasses, and I realised that I was frowning too, a mirror image.

"How are you today, Mildred?" I said. I wanted to offer more, to reassure her, but couldn't think of anything to say. Instead, in silence, I put my hand to her cheek and ran my fingers along her wrinkles. Cold and weak like wet paper. I breathed in her breath. It was a disgusting smell, but with a subtle note of compost sweetness.

I brought the food syringe to her lips. She closed them and pulled her head back.

"You have to eat," I said, "or you'll never get well."

"No, no," she said, distinctly.

"Mildred," I said, and gently held her chin while I squeezed half the contents of the syringe into her mouth. She coughed and turned her head away, spitting the food out onto her quilt. Her breath rattled now – it sounded like sucking a straw in an almost-empty glass of water.

I took a cloth out of my pocket and mopped up the spilt food. Then I grabbed her jaw, firmly this time, hard enough to leave two burgundy bruises. She tried to clench her teeth, but I forced them apart with the plastic nib of the syringe. She opened her eyes stretch-wide, and stared at me as I squeezed the rest of the food down her throat.

Half an hour later, I was watching TV on my own in the lounge when an assistance alarm went off. I glanced over to the board; it was coming from Mildred's room.

When I got there I saw that it was Dani who had pressed the button. "Mildred's carked it," she said. She took off Mildred's glasses and closed her eyes with her thumb and forefinger. "Help me get her on the bed."

I walked up to the armchair and put my hand on Mildred's shoulder. "Her neck's already hard," I said, "like rigor mortis."

"Reckon it's the draught what's done it," said Dani, and she leaned over to shut the window.

We threw off Mildred's quilts and heaved her onto the bed. She looked like she should weigh no more than a screwed-up ball of paper, but she was surprisingly heavy.

"I'll call the doctor to declare it, you finish putting Dennis to bed. He's toileting right now," instructed Dani, and she left the room.

I lingered. I had never seen a real dead person before. I wanted to say something to her, but it felt inappropriate. I watched her for a minute, then picked up the quilts from the floor and covered her.

I perched on the bed next to her, put my fingers against her tiny wrist and held them there. I could swear I felt a pulse, but maybe it was my own. I looked at the boxes and photos on her dressing table. What would happen to all her stuff? I wondered. Would any of her family show up to claim it?

One of the photos, black and white, was of a young woman on a pony, her plaid skirt billowing in the wind. Another was of a soldier, stern and handsome, looking up as if he saw the future.

It was easy to think of the residents as something less than human. Mrs Thwaite the rectal prolapse, Dennis the alcoholic, Floris the manic depressive. They were caricatures. Dolls that you dressed and undressed, and when undressed they looked less like people and more like warted gourds.

Mildred was a human being. For eighty years she strove and loved and wanted and searched for meaning. And she had ended up here. The last voice she ever heard was mine, a total stranger's.

I had loved her. But I didn't really know her. There must have been people out there who did. They would never know about me. That I dressed and undressed her. That I cleaned her when she pissed herself. That I confessed my darkest fears to her because she couldn't understand. That I was sitting next to her, feeling her wrist for a pulse.

I felt deeply ashamed.

I handed in my notice a week later. I hadn't realised how much I loved working there until Mildred died and I stopped enjoying it at all. I couldn't look Dani in the eye when I told her I was leaving. I haven't spoken to her, or any of them, since then.

First published in The Mechanics' Institute Review Issue 7 (Birkbeck, 2010)

Mildred is based on a real person. While at university (in the early '00s), working at a care home, hers was the first dead body I ever saw – and I was surprised by my overriding emotion.

Guilt.

The moment stuck with me, and in 2009, for my creative writing master's degree at Birkbeck, I wrote this story in an attempt to make sense of why I'd felt that way. Re-reading it still makes me cry.

SCHRÖDINGER'S BABY

"

*I don't know if I've got an alive baby
or a dead baby until I can open this
bloody door!*

There she slept, a puckered little bundle of DNA fighting to organise. She looked and smelled like a lump of dough. Her breathing rattled less than it had when she was born; I could hardly tell she was alive apart from that relentless ticking.

There was an electronic pad tucked beneath her baby mattress that sensed her breathing, translating each inhalation and exhalation into a metronomic tick. The ticks were supposed to be reassuring, but to me they sounded like a countdown.

Everything about the last year had been a countdown. Waiting to conceive, watching the bump grow, buying everything we thought we needed. At each stage I was convinced that the hidden timer would reach zero, and Elaine would get bored of our workaday lives, escape back to the wealth she'd been accustomed to. Even after the birth, the countdown seemed to continue. I stared at the baby, waiting to feel something. Tick. Tick. Tick.

She wasn't born, technically, rather pulled from Elaine's stomach like a weed. That's where Elaine was now, having her stitches tended, having her shredded dignity prodded into further submission.

I told the baby I loved her, trying to believe it.

Coffee. I went to the kitchen and prepared a really strong cup. But we were out of milk. The shop was next door to our flat; I could be out and back before the coffee cooled. Cursing, I grabbed the ticking intercom from the lounge and went out.

"Hi, Mo," I said to the Indian guy behind the counter as I entered the corner store. It wasn't always the same guy, but as far as I could gather they were all called Mo.

"Hello, Mister Franks. How is your little girl?"

I held up the ticking intercom. "Still alive."

"This is the best age, ah? You can gaze at them all day. I have seven daughters, you know. Can't stop myself."

"Really?" I said, distracted. What had I come in for? I hadn't been getting much sleep.

"They are very difficult when they grow. Our oldest – twelve years – she is chatting about eye-phones and Myspacebook and popping music. We have no idea what she is talking about."

"I always wanted a child," I said. "But I'm not sure I want an infant."

I rubbed my face. Milk – that's what I'd come in for. I grabbed the biggest bottle. Elaine called these six-pinters "the Cow". But when it came to paying,

I realised I didn't have my wallet. I grumbled under my breath, set down the Cow, and scurried out.

At the door to our building I patted my pockets. Patted them again. Looked down. I was wearing my pyjamas, the powder-blue ones Elaine's mother had given me for Christmas. I put the ticking intercom on the ground and, ridiculously, patted my pockets again.

Of course the keys weren't there. I knew exactly where they were – in my jeans, next to my bedside table. On the other side of two double-locked doors. In a last-ditch display of utter fantasy, I gave myself one last full-body pat-down before the panic started to set in. A prickle at the back of my neck; a tinge of whiteness in my vision. I contained it and willed myself to think. My first instinct was to walk away, pretend the baby didn't exist, and live the rest of my life under a bridge.

Elaine's mother had a spare key. She lived just a few bus stops away. I could call her and be there in ten minutes. But – no. I couldn't call her: my mobile was also in the pocket of my jeans.

Back to the shop.

"Hello again, Mister Franks. You forgot something?"

"Mo, have you got a phone I could use?"

"Not for customers, sorry."

"Please, it's an emergency."

"*Ji*? Problem with your little one?"

"No, it's, uh ... it's ... Can I use your phone please?"

Mo must have seen something in my face. He handed over his mobile. But I had no idea what number to dial. I called Elaine instead, the only number I could remember.

"Hello? Who's this?"

I felt a blush of warmth, an abdominal tug.

"Elaine, it's me. How're you doing?"

"Still waiting. You know how it is with hospitals. Waiting, waiting, waiting. How's the baby?"

"I'm just calling . . ." Why was I calling? What was I doing? Elaine had entrusted me with the baby and I was about to admit that I was the worst father in the world?

"What number is this?" she asked.

"The baby's fine. She's asleep."

"I miss her." Her voice became shaky. "Sorry, still feeling a bit fragile."

"I just . . . What's your mother's number? I wanted to call her to . . . thank her for those pyjamas. I'm wearing them now."

I made a frantic scribbling gesture towards Mo, who took a few seconds to realise I was asking for a pen. I scrawled the number onto the back of my hand, filled the air with sweet platitudes, and hung up.

"That did not sound like an emergency," said Mo.

"Shut up, Mo."

I dialled Elaine's mother's number.

"Hello?"

"Mrs Leclerc, it's –"

"Daniel! What a surprise. How lovely to hear from you. How's my gorgeous granddaughter? She is simply the most ravishingly beautiful baby I have ever set eyes on. She gets it from me, darling."

"She's fine."

"She's fine, he says. Men are always so articulate on such matters. My husband –"

"Mrs Leclerc, I wonder if you can help me."

"Ah! Seeking some parental advice? Well, you've come to exactly the right place. You only need to look at how wonderfully well-mannered Elaine is to see –"

"Do you have our spare set of keys?"

"Yes, dear. You endowed us with responsibility for them and we've taken that responsibility seriously. They're in the jewellery box at the back of the cutlery drawer."

"Could you please bring them over? Or can I come and get them?"

"I'm in Brighton, dear. The Conservative conference. It would take me an hour at least to get home, and Sebastian's away on business, in Monaco. Is it an emergency?"

I gritted my teeth.

"Darling?" she prompted.

"No. Sorry to bother you."

I hung up.

Mo glanced at the baby's ticking intercom, which I'd left on the countertop, and then looked sideways at me, grinning. "You're in a bit of a pickle, aren't you?"

I could feel the panic spreading in my veins like a poison. I wanted to shout, lash out. Instead, I closed my eyes, took a deep breath. My hands shook with the effort of containment.

"Mo, have you got the number of an emergency locksmith?"

Mo shrugged.

"I'll call directory enquiries." I held up the phone. "If you don't mind?"

Mo made a concessionary gesture. His lips clenched as if suppressing a smirk.

I got numbers for two locksmiths, and called the nearer one. "Hello," I said when a man with meticulous received pronunciation answered. "I've locked my keys in my flat and I need someone to come and let me in. It's urgent."

"Certainly," said the man. "We charge £250 for changing locks, and a £50 call-out fee."

"Fine, fine." I told him my address.

"We can be there in ten minutes. Do you have a form of identification?"

"No. My wallet's in the flat."

"A driver's licence? A utility bill?"

"I'm in my pyjamas."

Mo leaned over, cupping a hand to his mouth. "Very nice pyjamas they are too!" I elbowed him out of the way.

"I'm afraid we can't change the locks unless you can provide valid identification showing your address."

I tried not to let my irritation show. Unsuccessfully. "I can provide ID as soon as you let me into my flat."

"I'm sorry, sir," came the snitty reply. "I'm afraid we can't help you." He hung up.

I let out a primal roar. Mo looked concerned that I might cast his phone into the liquor aisle. I swallowed my rage and stabbed in the number of the second locksmith.

"Hello, Securelock Limited."

"Hi. I'm locked out of my flat."

"Right. I can sort that out for you, no problem."

"It's an emergency. And I don't have any identification."

"What's the address?"

I told him.

"I'm on another call at the moment, sir, so I can be with you in . . . say . . . forty-five minutes."

I checked my watch. My face must have been a picture – Mo actually looked sorry for me. "Can't you come any faster?"

"Forty-five minutes."

I sighed tensely, hung up, and handed over the phone, blinking back a tear. "Thanks, Mo."

"My name is actually Sukhvinder."

I picked up the plastic intercom from the countertop. It wasn't ticking any more. I shook it. Held it to my ear, straining to listen. Popped the back open and rolled the batteries around. Nothing.

"Batteries, batteries!" I barked.

Mo fumbled, spilling several packs of batteries onto the countertop as he reached up for them. I grabbed one, ripped it open. Levered out the old batteries and shoved in the new ones. Nothing.

I checked and double-checked. The batteries were in correctly, the intercom was switched on, the volume was turned up, yet there was no sound. I looked up at Mo. His eyebrows formed an inverted V. He covered his mouth with his hand.

I ran out of the shop and banged on our front door. I rattled the handle, uselessly, then stepped back and ran at it like a battering ram. Mo came out of the shop to watch as I banged at the door again and again like a wasp against a window. It wasn't going to budge.

I stopped. Tried to think rationally. Failed. "Mo, help!"

Mo shrugged. "Do not to go crazy. Probably she scooched off the sensor or it has malfunctioned."

"I don't know if I've got an alive baby or a dead baby until I can open this bloody door!"

I looked up at the windows. Our flat is on the first floor. An old Victorian metal drainpipe led up past the nursery window. I clamped myself to it and tried to shimmy my way up.

Turns out that kind of thing is only possible in cartoons. The drainpipe was rusty and flaky, and in my effort to gain purchase I managed to pull it off the wall. A stinking slosh of stagnant water landed on my face. I spluttered and retched as the pipe arced gracefully down, twisted to one side, and landed heavily on my neighbour's Subaru Impreza, popping out the passenger-side window.

I stared at the car, my shoulders jerking with dry sobs that were almost laughter. It was parked near the porch; now that the drainpipe lay across the front of the house it might be possible to climb from the top of the car up onto the roof of the porch.

I jumped onto the car, denting the hood, then reached up to the broken pipe. Hanging, hand over hand, I worked my way up. I tried to haul myself onto the porch roof, but the drainpipe bowed. "Mo!" I shouted. "Give me a leg up!"

Mo glanced nervously at the door of his shop, then slunk over and held up his hands. I stepped on them, then onto his turban, and heaved myself onto the porch roof.

Leaning precariously over the edge, using a stretch of broken drainpipe for support, I stared into the nursery window. I could see her, just, but there was no way of telling whether she was moving. Never before had I appreciated what it meant to have a lump in your throat, but now I felt like I'd swallowed a lemon.

Directly over the porch was the lounge window. I braced myself and kicked. It resonated loudly, but didn't break. I wound myself up for a firmer kick, and nearly slipped off the roof with shock when a siren sounded not ten metres behind me.

I crouched on all fours to keep my balance. Cautiously, I turned my head to see a policeman stepping out of his vehicle. From the corner of my eye I saw Mo slip quietly back into the store.

"Hold it," shouted the cop.

"This is my house! I need to get my baby!" At least that's what I intended to say. It came out a little garbled.

"Down. Right now," ordered the policeman. "We'll discuss it at the station." He yelled more orders and threats, but I could only hear the rush of blood in my ears. I turned back to the window and gave it a powerful kick.

My foot went through the glass. The sound was surprising, a staccato of hollow ringing. Even more surprising was that when I retrieved my leg, a large triangle of glass came with it, embedded in my calf.

I staggered, reaching out for something to hold on to, but my leg gave way beneath me. As I fell, I saw every mistake I'd ever made, and I had just enough time to register that none of them had been as bad as this one.

THWACK. The pavement tasted salty metallic. I blacked out.

*

I woke with a start. Horizontal. Tried to get to my feet, but my leg was braced and my head felt like someone had stuffed it full of nails. I squinted my eyes to try and focus. I was in hospital. Without the baby.

A pressure built up on my chest, and kept building, like a marching band trampling my ribcage. It grew into a full-on military tattoo. I was officially the worst father – no, the worst person – in the world. If I was on a life-support machine, it should be switched off now.

"Please try to relax." The voice belonged to a robust-looking female doctor. "You're in King's College Hospital Emergency Department being treated for shock, head trauma, a broken leg and a partially severed Achilles tendon. You'll be all right, but you need to settle down."

I tried to say something, but my voice sounded like it was coming from somewhere else and I lost my train of speech.

"Calm down or you'll do yourself more damage. Stop moving about and tell me your name."

I looked up at the doctor with pleading wet eyes.

"What is your name?" She enunciated every syllable.

I concentrated, struggling to cut through the morphine mist. "Dan. Yel. Franks."

"Daniel Franks?"

I nodded. "My . . . baby . . ."

"Can we contact someone for you?"

"My baby my baby my baby!"

The doctor's face tightened with concern. "I'll be right back, OK Daniel?"

"No!" I bawled, but she'd already left. I needed to concentrate. I needed to speak to someone. I had to get to a phone. I searched my bedside for an emergency pull-cord, thinking that this couldn't possibly get any worse. Then it got worse.

A familiar figure loomed above me, leaning on a crutch. My heart swelled and fluttered. It was Elaine, wearing a hospital gown. I gawked at her helplessly. She looked crestfallen.

"Oh, Danny," she said. "I was just about to have my check-up and I got a call saying you were here. Oh, honey . . ."

I wanted to gouge my eyes out with a spoon. "I'm . . . sorry, Elaine – so sorry . . . The baby –" The word caught in my throat and came out as a kind of hiccough.

"You must have been terrified. Sukhvinder told me all about it."

Sukhvinder?

Then I saw him. Mo – Sukhvinder – standing behind Elaine. In his arms, a tiny miracle. My precious doughy baby. He winked at me. "I called your wife on my mobilephone and told her about the *bewakoof* burglar who broke your window and attacked you while you were responsibly babysitting."

Elaine leaned over and stroked my hair. "I don't know how you had the presence of mind to drag yourself downstairs and ask Sukhvinder for help. Or should I say: Mo." She flashed me a wry smile and kissed me on the forehead. I sank back into the crisp hospital sheets; felt like I was floating.

Gingerly, Mo bent down and placed the baby on my chest. He lingered a moment to whisper in my ear. "The locksmith arrived. I took the baby and called your wife from my last-dialled numbers." He straightened up, then ducked down again to whisper one last thing. "You owe me three hundred fifty for the locksmith. And four pound ninety-nine for batteries."

But I barely heard him. I stared at the baby wriggling on my chest. She glowed with life. The thought that I might have lost her – that I might ever lose her – filled me with butterfly panic. She was small and perfect, yet so precarious. I caressed her yielding fontanelle, weeping with joy and apprehension.

First published in The Mechanics' Institute Review Issue 10 (Birkbeck, 2013)

In 2011, I became a father, and a year later I wrote this story. Any connection between the two events is pure speculation.

The flat and the corner shop are based on where we lived in Brixton – opposite the skate park, just round the corner from where David Bowie grew up. I loved that place. The struggle with locksmiths is inspired by one of my favourite short stories: Fernando Sorrentino's A Lifestyle.

CULTURE SCULPTOR

*I'm a God-fearin' man, but there are
one or two people I fear more.*

In my dream I ran down a corridor, which extended
endlessly before me. The school bell was ringing
and I knew I was late for class. I woke up with a
headache and it took two more rings of the phone
before I realised where I was. Slumped in my tiny
West Hollywood office, drooling onto my sport coat.

I was too old to be having dreams about school. My
subconscious was trapped in the Sixties. Not the trippy
happy Sixties that it's fashionable to mythologise –
all that kind of stuff was happening to other people.

The Nineties suit me better. Everyone else is
miserable too.

I picked up the phone. "Hello?"

"Am ah speaking to Mistuh Haams?" A low Southern
drawl.

"Ted Himes," I said, rubbing my forehead. "Yes."

"Ah understand that you specialise in finding lost
people. Ah can't give you a lot to go on, but ah can
pay you well for success. However, ah desire the

utmost discretion. There must be no ripples in the lake, y'understand?"

"Of course. I have an excellent track record of dealing with extremely sensitive cases."

"Ah'm a God-fearin' man, Mistuh Haams, but there are one or two people ah fear more."

I made reassuring noises. Specifically, I told him I was the best damn private eye this side of the Sierra Nevada. In truth, any hint of danger made me wring my tie like I was trying to get milk out of it.

"Ah don't mean to patronise you, Mistuh Haams, but ah fear for my life already and ah don't want you gettin' involved unless you understand that pursuing this case might put you in the firing line."

My tie was getting pretty creased. But a paycheque's a paycheque. I cleared my throat. "Would you like to come to my office to discuss it, or would you prefer a more anonymous location?"

"Ah like your thinking, Mistuh Haams. Consider yourself hired. Ah'll be there in twenty seconds."

The phone clicked off. I leapt up and pulled the window blind aside just in time to see an overweight man with a trucker hat and a briefcase leave the phone booth and walk into my building. I panicked, trying to mop up the patch of drool from my lapel with one hand while ironing the creases out of my tie with the other.

When the knock came I tried to look natural, but I'm a much better actor over the phone than in person.

He was large and he smelled of fresh sweat, but he moved with surprising grace. He sat firmly; I asked him if he wanted a drink and he politely refused.

"Ah'd like t'get straight t'business. Forgive me for not introducing myself but ah'm going to great pains to ensure that you and ah can never be connected, exceptin' this meeting of course. You'll be better off that way."

"Who is it that you'd like me to find?" I asked, offering him a cigarette. He refused it, so I swallowed the urge to light up myself.

He opened his briefcase and passed me a black-and-white eight by ten – a convoy of old cars with a crowd looking on. One of the faces in the foreground of the crowd was circled in red marker. It took me a few seconds to realise what I was looking at. It was an angle I hadn't seen before, but it was unmistakeable.

"That's JFK," I said, pointing to the President's smiling face in the leading vehicle.

My client nodded. "Minutes before he was shot."

I seriously considered pigeonholing this guy as a conspiracy nut. I tried to control my expression. "And you want me to find a random onlooker? Three decades later?"

"Not a random onlooker. A witness." He tapped his finger on the red circle. "What's more, ah've seen this man with my own eyes. Twice, back home in Memphis. Once, leaving rooms on Mulberry on April fourth 1968, right after Martin Luther King was shot.

And again nearly ten years later, leaving Graceland on August sixteenth 1977."

Pigeon thoroughly holed. "You're a conspiracy nut."

"Hear me out. Ah recognised this man on that day in '77, and ah followed him, even before I knew Elvis Presley had just died. It was sheer dumb luck that ah was nearby for the death of King and, uh, the King. Ah'm a lifelong Memphian, but of all the people in Memphis, ah think ah might be the only one who could've made the link."

I rubbed my forehead. "What's this got to do with Kennedy?"

"Like ah say, ah followed that man, mostly on a hunch. Ah found out where he was staying, what name he was staying under. Ah hung out in the bar, hopin' he'd come down for some conversation. But ah never saw him."

"So? You were there for both deaths too, and you admit it was coincidence."

"Something about the way he carried himself. Like he didn't care. Ah believed it was no coincidence. Ah tried to track him. Soon enough ah figured he'd been using a fake name, and that truly got me going. Ah'm afraid ah became a little obsessed with trying to find him. The more ah found out, the more ah suspected."

"And you're still looking after eighteen years?" I asked.

"Ah've found out more'n you know," he said, fixing me with his wet eyes. "More'n it's safe to know. Ah don't wish to burden you with it. All ah can give you is this picture, an old one but the only one ah have of him, and a list of aliases he's used. Ah have reason to believe he lives here in California, and works for someone nearby. Ah need you to find out where he is. Anything you can about him."

"Based on this?"

"The information is reliable."

"Even if it is, this is lightweight. Could take weeks."

He sat back and mopped sweat from his face. "What're your rates?" he asked.

I told him. He nodded, pulled out a chequebook and wrote me a cheque that equated to about a month's pay.

He handed it to me. "That's by way of a down payment." In trembling silence he wrote a second cheque for ten times the amount, but postdated this one by two months. He signed it and handed it to me. "Mistuh Haams." He chewed on the words. "You'll see that ah'm quite serious about this. Ah'm putting my trust in you."

He slid a blank envelope towards me and motioned for me to open it. It contained a key.

"When ah walk out this door ah will never see you again," he continued, leaning forward and enunciating as if to say he would not invite questions. "In exactly one month's time ah will check the safety deposit box at the Bank of America on North La Brea, for which you now have the only other key. If it's empty, ah will cancel that second cheque. It will not be empty."

For that, I will humour you, I thought, fingering the second cheque. "I understand," I said. "I'll find him, and I won't ask any questions."

"God bless, and be careful."

*

I closed up the office and worked on the case full time, running all the aliases through the usual checks for California addresses, then again for Tennessee. Post office records, court records, phone records, the DMV, city directories and county recorders. Tax. Voter registrations. The works. Not hard if you know where to look, but very time consuming. You need a lot of patience in my job.

My therapist tells me that I became a private investigator to prove something to my parents. I left home – ran away, I guess – when I was fifteen, and didn't speak to my mom and dad for ten years. So now I spend every waking hour finding people to prove that they could have found me if they wanted to. That's what my therapist says. I say it's the best job for a man who wants to keep to himself in a city like LA.

I worked on the case day and night. It took me the best part of three weeks before I had enough information to start making some helpful deductions. But this guy used every trick in the book to keep himself hard to find. A professional. I had to stay focused, and trust my instincts. If something smells fishy, beware red herring.

I'd narrowed down his most commonly used aliases; I was pursuing a hunch that his real name was Chase

Lytton. I looked up all the Chase Lyttons in California, past and present. There were five that I could find. Two were easy to trace, two were dead, and the last one proved extremely hard to pin down.

I was pretty sure I had my man.

By that time my month was almost up. I still hadn't worked out Mr Lytton's exact location, but now that I'd figured out who he was it was only a matter of time. I just needed to keep my eye on all the usual channels and he'd give himself away eventually. No one can stay off the grid forever unless they hole up in a tent for the rest of their lives, and this guy was no Wilderness Explorer.

I typed up a note to that effect, bundled it up with a summary of the evidence I'd gathered, and headed for my client's safety deposit box on La Brea Avenue. It was one of those semi-private affairs where there's a little booth for you to open your box in. I showed the key to the attendant and she brought me out a metal box about ten by twelve inches on top and six inches deep.

I expected the box to be empty, but it wasn't. There was an envelope on top with my name on it, in uneven handwriting. Underneath the envelope was a tattered old file, thick with documents, clippings and photographs that spilled out from the edges. The cover was so worn it looked like it would fall apart if I touched it.

The envelope contained a hastily handwritten letter, dated almost one month ago – the day my client had visited me. I could hear his Memphis accent as I read it.

Mister Himes, by the time you read this I will be dead. Assassinated by the man I asked you to find. I can only hope that the same fate does not await you. I'm afraid I misled you when we spoke. There aren't two keys for this box. I gave you the only one, and with it my life's work for the last 18 years. This evidence took me years to deduce, but will take you only a few days to independently verify. I hope that once you absorb the contents of this file you will appreciate their importance, and you will choose to continue my work. I'm counting on you to succeed where I have failed. Your investigations so far will give you some idea of how elusive and cunning this man can be. God bless, and be careful.

I flattened out my tie.

West Hollywood is an uneasy kind of area to walk through at the best of times, but I've never looked over my shoulder as often as I did on the way back to my office with that mysterious file under my arm.

It took me several hours to comprehend the contents of that file, and their implications. By four in the morning I'd started rereading the whole thing for the third time and I knew I should head home, but frankly I was a little nervous about leaving the office. I knew in my bones that people had been killed to protect this information. My client included.

When I woke up, splayed across my office chair, the file and its secrets were still in front of me like a tumour lodged in my brain. I thought about the fat cheque the Memphian had left me, and considered throwing the file in the trash – living the quiet life for a few months. But even as I considered, I knew this secret was too big to ignore. I'd promised to try and find Chase Lytton, so try I would.

I read the file once more. The contents were arranged more or less chronologically, providing evidence as to the whereabouts of Chase Lytton, often under an alias, at various times over the last thirty years. Sometimes there were big gaps, and there were occasional chapters that were somewhat more speculative, but for the most part the evidence was remarkably robust.

Mr Lytton, it seemed, had witnessed the death of a frightening number of celebrities and media personalities over the years. He had been present, or at least nearby, when Elvis Presley died, when Martin Luther King was shot, and when John F Kennedy was killed. But also when Buddy Holly's plane crashed; when Marilyn Monroe overdosed; when Jimi Hendrix took too much Vesparax; when Bruce Lee suffered his fatal allergic reaction. Janis Joplin. Jim Morrison. John Lennon. River Phoenix. Kurt Cobain. The list went on.

No conclusions were drawn, but the facts were compelling. One man had attended all of these tragedies. The common theme was that each of these famous people had died before their time, usually under circumstances that were not entirely clear. No claim was being made that Mr Lytton killed these people himself – in one or two instances there was even evidence that proved he hadn't – but he was there. It was far beyond a coincidence. Something extremely strange was afoot, and it made me squirm in my chair.

The file could have been a hoax of Rube Goldberg proportions, but it didn't make sense. All the same, I knew I had to check the facts to be sure. If it was fake, I'd be able to see through it easily, but my instincts told me that this file – collated over so many years – spoke the truth.

Now, I'm no hero. When danger rears its ugly head I'd rather be sipping a scotch in a bar on the other side of town. So over the next few days while I verified the facts, I became unbearably paranoid. I started wearing shades, even after sunset. I walked home a different way each day. I put a sliver of tape on the frame of my apartment door, and every window, so I could see if someone had been in while I'd been away. Same with the office. I woke up in the middle of the night, dreaming that I'd seen the tell-tale red pinpoint of light from a rifle sight on my chest, or that there was a poisonous thread dangling into my mouth like in a Bond film. Then I started relying on the strongest pills I could get my hands on just to be able to get to sleep at all.

Who was Chase Lytton? I tried to think of a rational explanation, but rationality evaded me. Could he be a clairvoyant journalist? Some kind of angry Martian? In my mind he grew and warped into something preternatural, a vengeful angel of death, and every time I looked over my shoulder I expected to see his glowing eyes boring a hole into my soul.

Undoubtedly those stressful days shaved a few years off my life, not least because I went up to forty cigarettes a day, but as it turns out my paranoia saved me.

I'd been verifying the information in the file in approximately reverse chronological order. I'd got to about 1975, and it was getting harder as the records got older, but so far everything checked out. It was past midnight, I'd been up and working since four in the morning, so I decided to call it a day and head home.

As had become my habit, when I got to my apartment I checked the sliver of tape I'd stuck on the frame of the front door that morning. It was broken. I came out in an instant sweat that felt like a thousand tiny knives. My heart beat in my throat. For the first time in my life, I wished I had a gun.

My instinct was to turn tail and flee, but where would I go? He knew where I was. I wasn't safe anywhere. I swallowed hard, breathed deeply. Borrowed a brass ornament from my neighbour's planter. Quietly tried the door; it was locked. I unlocked it and went inside.

The fist-sized brass Buddha shook in my upraised hand as I jerked from room to room. Hall – empty. Kitchen – empty. Diner – empty. Bedroom – empty. Bathroom – empty. No signs of intrusion. Nothing seemed to be missing. If someone had been in here, they were extremely careful to leave things as they'd found them.

My spine suddenly surged with another burst of adrenalin. The file! I crashed out of the apartment, and ran back to the office. When I got there I was retching for breath. My lungs were killing me. My hand was shaking so much it took minutes to get the key in the lock.

I slammed open the door. The file was still there – it hadn't been stolen. I dropped to my knees, then collapsed into a ball. I felt physically sick with the burden of fear and responsibility. I cried for a few minutes, leaking snot and dignity onto my Furniture Vision rug. Got it out of my system.

When I'd calmed down and cleaned myself up, I resolved that in the morning I'd make copies of the file and send them anonymously to every newspaper in Los Angeles. Then I'd take the damn thing to the nearest police station and hand it over. Wash my hands of it. Feeling marginally better, I gathered up the file, shoved it under my arm and went home.

By the time I got to bed I'd almost managed to convince myself that it was probably the landlady who'd come in during the day. I'd ask her in the morning, I thought, feeling faintly ridiculous. I popped my last couple of sleeping pills, vexed that I'd emptied another bottle already. As I drifted off, I thought of Jimi Hendrix and Marilyn Monroe, loved by the world, dying alone in their sleep.

My eyes shot open. Suddenly I knew how half the people in that file had died.

I rolled off the bed and forced a finger down my throat. Vomited on the floor. Just managed to crawl my way to the phone and dial 911 before I passed out.

*

When I woke up in hospital, with a splitting headache and spots dancing before my eyes, my suspicions were confirmed. I'd taken a massive overdose of sleeping pills. The only reason I was still alive was because I'd vomited them up before my system had fully absorbed them. The doctors said I must have taken the whole bottle. But I'd taken two pills.

Things clicked together. Someone really had broken into my apartment. The perfect way to commit murder and make it seem like suicide or an accidental overdose. All those celebrities had been assassinated by Chase Lytton, or at least under his supervision. Never suspecting a thing. Never leaving a trace.

Mr Lytton was no angel of death. He was nothing supernatural. He was a disgusting, calculating, homicidal human being. The greatest serial killer in history. An unparalleled psychopath. He'd taken a shot at me, but I'd survived. I'd survived, and it was my destiny to stop him.

I was weak, but felt energised. Fear and paranoia sublimated into anger and determination. I discharged myself as soon as the doctors said I was past danger. My ideas of handing this over to the press and the police vanished. Now, this was personal. And, what's more, I had a lead. A thin one, but a lead all the same, and I intended to pursue it to whatever end.

The brand of sleeping pills I'd been using was Ambien. A glance at the side of the bottle told me that the main active ingredient was a chemical called zolpidem tartrate. There were no pills left in the bottle; I'd taken the last two. Of course – my would-be assassin wouldn't want to leave behind pills that could be tested and proven to be doctored. It had to appear as if I'd taken an overdose under my own steam.

Manufacturing bent pills to order wasn't trivial. There had to be a limited number of suppliers and buyers of zolpidem. I didn't know how to get that information, but that's where I had to begin. I guessed it would be a slog, but that's what I'm good at. Mr Lytton would be watching and plotting another hit so I had to be smart and act fast.

While I did my research I became intentionally unpredictable. I ate in a different fast-food joint for every meal. Slept in different beds. I'd hole up in a café and use a public phone one day, then walk to midtown and work from a library the next. In short, I tried to keep myself hard to kill. I knew he'd catch up with me eventually, if he wanted to, but I wasn't going to make it easy.

Part of me was bothered that it would have been so easy to off me. I probably wouldn't have been found for days. I'm a man who likes to keep himself to himself, but my brush with death made me realise that my funeral would be like the reception party at a moon landing. I made a promise to myself to give my parents a call when this was done, then I tried to put the thought out of my mind.

I started by visiting the patent office. An officious young lady, who used her designer glasses as a weapon for condescension, made me wait three hours then told me that the patent on zolpidem was owned by a French company called Sanofi. I dialled Directory Assistance to get the number for Sanofi's US offices. They were in New Jersey.

A perky female voice answered the phone. "Sanofi switchboard, where can I direct you?"

"Hi, my name is Fred Limes. I'm the manager of the Chemical Supply and Licensing department at Bayer. I wonder if you can help me. I attended a conference last month and met someone from Sanofi that I'd really like to talk to, only I can't remember his name. What's the equivalent department over there?"

"Oh, I'm not sure. Hang on a moment and I'll look it up for you." She put me on hold. An angry woman yodelled something about jagged little pills for a minute or two. "Hello? I think you need the Clinical Supply Chain Directorate, sir."

"Thank you. Who's the director there?"

"Um . . . Chad Barker, sir."

"Hm. No, that wasn't him. Who else is in that team?"

"Isaac Bukowski, Ken Nelson, Larry Martinez . . ." She gave me a few more names, which I frantically scribbled down, until I pretended to recognise one. I showered her with gratitude and told her to have a wonderful day. Now I had a list of people I could call to try and get more information.

I called back from a different phone, using a different voice. "Can I speak to Isaac Bukowski please?"

The operator put me through.

"Isaac Bukowski speaking."

"Hello Mr Bukowski. Do you have a few minutes to spare?"

"Who's speaking?"

"I'm Mr Grisham," I said. "A friend of mine gave me your number. I'm researching a book, set in the pharmaceutical industry, and I'd be so grateful if I could ask you a few questions. If you can spare the time."

There was a pause. "Is this John Grisham? The author?"

"I'll only take a few minutes of your time. You'll get a special thanks at the back of the book if I use the material. But until then, you'll understand if I ask you to be discreet."

"Of course. Yeah. I'd love to help. Just a sec, I'll find a quiet spot."

Hook, line and sinker. I wouldn't always get this lucky, so I went straight for the jugular. "I'm trying to understand a bit about the pharmaceutical supply chain. I'm not familiar with a lot of the jargon so it'd be great if you could really break it down for me. Perhaps you could use a specific example that'd help me visualise it. Like Ambien. That's one of yours isn't it?"

"Oh yeah, but I do cardiovasculars. But I can talk you through how things work."

I heard him out, asking as many questions as I thought I could get away with. Then I used that knowledge to call the next guy on the list with a different ruse. And so on, again and again, until I knew quite a bit about the workings of Sanofi's supply chain. In particular, I knew how drugs like zolpidem were manufactured, licensed and sold. The good news for me was that the exact manufacturing process was a profitable secret, and therefore closely guarded. So no one could get their hands on it without Sanofi being involved, especially at short notice.

Now I knew what questions to ask and who would know the answer. But they wouldn't just gift-wrap me a list of what zolpidem they'd sold to whom, whatever scam I used. So I needed a new tactic. I called up an old acquaintance. A senior investigator at the FBI who occasionally helps me out, if he's got out of the right side of bed.

"Bob, good to hear your voice," I said when he answered.

"What do you want, Ted?"

"Not even a how are you?"

"I don't want to ask you how you are. You might tell me. Then I'd be depressed for the rest of the day."

"Point taken. I need to call in a favour."

"What favour? You're about four favours in debt."

"You're going to arrange a little corporate disclosure for me." I told him what I needed.

"Are they implicated in a crime?"

"No. It's for a case of mine."

"You won't even tell me what it's for? Are you insane?"

"Listen –"

"No way. Not a chance. Way too risky."

"It's urgent. Very, very urgent. I could offer you some . . . incentive."

His hand covered the phone for a moment. Then he half whispered, "How much?" The way he said it implied that he would need a lot.

I sighed. Reached into my inside pocket and pulled out the huge cheque that the fat man from Memphis had given me. It was still postdated by just over a week. I flipped it over and wrote on the back: Pay to the order of Bob Poston.

I told him how much. He said he would do it. I signed the endorsement.

The result was faxed to me two days later. A list of every single person in the country authorised to produce or purchase zolpidem, and how much they had got through in the last year. At the top of the list were various divisions of Sanofi itself, using tons of the stuff every month. Then there was a long tail of smaller manufacturers and distributors.

I started at the bottom and worked my way up, until I found what I was looking for. A company that hadn't needed zolpidem all year, except for a tiny order this month. The organisation was called C S (Pharma) Inc. and was registered in Tulare, California. That was it. I'd just found the pharmaceutical wing of my assassin's front organisation. A warm rush swelled through me; my brain felt like it was floating. Mr Lytton wasn't the only one who could be crafty.

A quick call to the SEC established that the company's director was one Donald Turnupseed. Turnupseed – where had I heard that name before? This was the man I needed to speak to. The man who could unravel the mystery of Chase Lytton.

Tulare was 150 miles away. Time for a drive.

*

The sun was setting as I arrived, tainting the tufted sky dirty pink like blood mixed with cotton candy. The address had taken me to a large warehouse on the outskirts of Tulare. Written on the building, as well as several trucks parked outside, was Turnupseed Electric Service. That name tickled something at the back of my mind, but I couldn't place it.

I rolled down the window. Diesel and ozone. The place looked like some kind of distribution centre. It seemed empty, closed up for the night. The back of my neck prickled; I felt uncomfortably conscious of my heartbeat. I parked up, grabbed the file and walked around the building.

On the far side one of the truck-sized roller doors was open. Inside there were two men leaning on the cab of a forty-foot rig, sharing a cigarette. I pulled out my pack and offered them fresh ones. The three of us lit up and puffed in silence for a moment.

"Can I help you?" asked the taller one. He had teeth the colour of saltwater taffy.

"Donald Turnupseed?" I inquired.

"Upstairs. Last office on the left," he said, pointing with his cigarette. He glanced at his watch. "But he usually goes home by eight."

"Hard worker. Thanks. I'll see if he's in."

My steps echoed on the metal stairs as I took them two at a time. The so-called offices looked more like shipping containers with doors cut into the side. The whole place reeked of cold efficiency. No creature comforts, no frills.

The door at the end of the walkway was labelled Donald Turnupseed in small, sober letters. I stubbed out my smoke, knocked twice and went straight in. The door closed behind me.

The office was sparse, but every item seemed carefully chosen. An expensive clock. Leather seats. An exotic plant. A black-and-white art print on the wall. And he was there, sitting behind a heavy-looking desk. A nameplate announced him as Donald Turnupseed, CEO.

"Who are you?" he barked. He was bald, thick glasses, big ears. Probably old enough to have retired. Everything about him looked starched.

"Mind if I smoke?" I asked, the next cigarette already on my lips.

"I do mind, sir. I had a lung tumour out last year. If you smoke you'll only tempt me. Mind you, it's not the cancer I'm afraid of; my wife would kill me."

I lit up. Took a long, slow drag.

"You are rude, sir," he said, taking off his glasses. "Have I offended you in some way?"

I hefted the file up and slammed it on his desk. I sat on one of his expensive leather chairs and watched him. He glared at me for a while. Then, eventually, he replaced his glasses and turned over the tattered front cover, holding it like it was a dirty napkin. He spent a few minutes slowly leafing through the articles, photos, letters, his face giving nothing away.

My cigarette finished; I threw the stub into the plant pot. "Who is Chase Lytton?"

Turnupseed stared at me like he was trying to set me on fire. He picked up his phone. I let him talk.

"Clive? It's Don. You still at the warehouse? Great, can you do me a – yep, that's right. Left it open again. I know, memory like a sieve. Thanks."

Turnupseed. That name. I'd read it before somewhere, and not on the side of a truck. As we sat there glowering at each other I dredged my brain. Something from long, long ago. A childhood memory. A sadness.

It clicked. Both my brain and the door. I remembered who Donald Turnupseed was, and at the same time the lock behind me clicked closed from the outside. I leapt out of my seat and tried the door. Banged on it for good measure. It wouldn't budge.

I kicked violently at the handle, crashed my shoulder against the door, but no use. My eyes darted around the office, which suddenly seemed claustrophobically small. There were no windows. No vents. No escape routes.

The corners of Turnupseed's tight lips rose. "You seem to know a lot about me," he said. "Or at least my work. So who are you?"

I grabbed his tie and pulled him across the desk, knocking off several stacks of paper and smashing his expensive clock. "Let me out!"

He put up an index finger, as if to silence me, leaned over and pressed the speaker button on his phone. The room filled with the sound of dial tone, then beeps as he dialled. I punched the phone, sending the receiver clattering to the floor.

"Ah ah. Break the phone and we'll be stuck in here all night."

I pulled his tie harder. He gurgled a little, but managed to maintain his composure. He twisted around to reactivate the speakerphone.

A gravelly voice answered. A deep, damaged voice like it came from a man who ate glass for breakfast. "Hello?"

"Chase," said Turnupseed. "I'm in my office. There's a man here who wants to meet you."

There was a pause. "Another?"

"I'm afraid so. How soon can you be here?"

A sigh. "Twenty minutes." He hung up.

Turnupseed leaned back and smiled cruelly. "There you go. You'll meet Chase in twenty minutes. Until then, we have the pleasure of each other's company."

"I could punch your lights out," I said.

"True," he countered. "But I don't have a key for that door. You'd still be stuck in here."

I pumped my fists. Twitched. Then felt the will drain out of me. Twenty minutes before Chase Lytton arrived to crack my skull like an egg. I slumped on the chair, deflated. Lit another cigarette.

The last time I'd seen Donald Turnupseed's name was on the front of a newspaper some forty years ago.

"You killed James Dean," I said. "That's where I've heard your name before. When I was a kid – six or maybe seven. You crashed into his Spyder with your Ford coupe."

"1955. I was twenty-three. Didn't see him. Damn nearly got killed myself."

"So who the hell is Chase Lytton?"

Turnupseed leaned forward. "There's crashes on that stretch of highway every day. Most of them get forgotten soon as they're cleaned up. But I happened to crash into James Dean. Do you know what it's like to get hate mail every day of your life for forty years? To have journalists calling your home and reminding you of a mistake you made half your life ago?"

"You went nuts."

"I picked myself up. Took over the family business and grew it into the biggest electrical contractors in the San Joaquin Valley. Raised four great kids. I'm a pillar of my community. Yet I only get remembered for one thing. The sad part about it is, no one appreciates what I did for James Dean. What I did for his millions of loving fans."

"What you did for them?"

"I made him what he is today. If he'd lived on he'd have faded into obscurity. But he's forever preserved at his peak, a golden boy, a teenage idol who can do no wrong. And by uniting in its worship and lamentation of him, society as a whole has been enriched by his passing."

I shifted in my seat. I felt crowded out by crazy. He kept talking.

"It got me to thinking. Maybe there's a formula. James Dean had the perfect balance of circumstances. Young, successful, admired, but with plenty of skeletons in his closet. Ripe for martyrdom. It was a service to kill him before his ugly side came out. Me and Chase talked for years about whether you could actually predict the optimum time to kill a celebrity in order to turn them into a cultural icon. Then we started doing it for real. We've been refining the formula ever since."

"For the benefit of society?"

"Absolutely. A cultural catharsis, if you will. I've made a more positive contribution to society than most presidents. These people were mediocre celebrities while they lived, but in their death they're born again – as heroes, idolised by the masses. They aren't victims, they're deities. Society rallies around their image, united by love and mourning. Far better than starting a war and uniting everyone by fear and hate, don't you think?"

"You've killed some of the most adored, most inspirational people of the twentieth century."

"I haven't killed anybody. I'm the brains. And the money, of course. Chase is the one who arranges the deaths. He finds the patsies, spreads the rumours that cloud the real cause of death. Some of the patsies even become famous in their own right. James Earl Ray. Lee Harvey Oswald. Roger Peterson was the first. He crashed the plane on the day the music died. They wrote a song about that."

"Anyone who has to hide what they're doing knows it's wrong."

"We've made mistakes. There's been a small amount of collateral damage. We left Elvis ten years too late. We only got Kennedy on the third try; that Pavlick bastard nearly gave us away. But for the most part, these people were freeze-framed in their prime, leaving a massive cultural legacy. Uniting the country – the world! Giving everyone a chance to let off steam in a positive direction for the sake of the social order. Our work is bigger than any one man. It's important. Chase is recruiting a cell of apprentices, to take over when we're gone, and I've endowed a generous trust fund. Hey, you want to know who's next? Sneak preview. We're going international. She hasn't passed the threshold yet, but I reckon it won't be long. The formula never lies. We're going to assassinate ourselves some British royalty."

I heard a click somewhere behind me and I spun round. The door banged open. I stumbled out of my chair as a figure dressed in black marched up to me and threw a bag over my head. I struggled like crazy but before I knew it he had my hands tied behind my back. I tried to squirm away but he'd tied me to something solid, tightly enough that I could feel the pulse in my wrists.

"Hello, Chase," said Turnupseed.

My breath caught as I panicked and bucked like a startled horse.

"I don't like having to kill snoops." That deathly voice, like tombstones rubbing together. "That's not what we signed up for."

"This'll be the last one," said Turnupseed. "He brought the Memphian's file with him. We can end this little distraction now."

I couldn't see anything through the bag, though I could hear them plainly enough.

I heard the distinctive hollow click of a gun chamber being loaded. A sound that traditionally makes me piss my pants. Every muscle in my body tensed as I braced for the feeling of the barrel against my temple, the cold finger of death.

"I plugged a new name into the formula," growled Chase. "And it came out way past the threshold. Long, long overdue."

"Really?" Turnupseed sounded excited. "Whose?"

"Yours."

A deafening bang made my eardrums ring. A startled cry.

I was disoriented. Light-headed. Minutes passed, or maybe seconds, before I was certain I hadn't been shot. I was somehow still intact.

I felt warm metal being pressed into my hand – a gun. Then suddenly my hands were loose. The bag came off my head and I turned just in time to see the door slip shut. I pulled it open and dived out to see Chase Lytton's back as he ran down the stairs, with the Memphian's file under his arm. I tried to go after him, but my legs were shaking.

It was already too late, but I aimed the gun at him and pulled the trigger. The chamber clicked empty. Then I realised why I was holding a gun. I was being framed. I rushed back into the office. Turnupseed had taken the bullet in his chest. Blood was bubbling out of the wound – the lung was punctured.

I did what I could for him, but I'm too squeamish for first aid; the only difference I made was to spread blood everywhere. I stepped back and took in the wrecked office, the almost dead man behind the desk, the gun on the floor with my fingerprints on it. It didn't look good.

I bolted.

*

The nature of Turnupseed's death was covered up. The papers reported that he'd had complications arising from his lung cancer. But the police knew how he'd died, and they were still looking for me.

He'd been right. Even in his death, Turnupseed's name was never published anywhere without being alongside James Dean's. If only those journalists had known how many other deaths he was responsible for. Who could I tell that would believe me?

Sure, if I had that file of evidence I could convince people, but it would take years to put it together again from scratch. I should have spent an extra day in the library making a copy, but I hadn't – I'd thought there was still time.

At times I was desperate to confide in someone, but that's exactly what Chase Lytton wanted. He wanted

Turnupseed to become a martyr, at my expense. His formula needed a patsy, a media catalyst, to make the guy into a cultural icon. I refused to give him the satisfaction.

I thought about Turnupseed a lot. Sometimes I didn't think of much else. I guess he was responding to a culture where people are constantly being built up to be brought down. Even if he could somehow calculate a net benefit to society, could the end ever justify the means?

Meanwhile, I was more alone than ever. I couldn't go back home, or back to my office, in case I got caught. I couldn't even stay in one place for too long. I wanted to call my parents, or anyone, but I'd caused them enough pain already. I carried the burden of a heavy secret that no one would believe, which made me feel yet more alone.

And it chilled me to know that Chase Lytton was still at large.

Two years later, in 1997, Princess Diana died in a car crash in Paris. The exact circumstances of the crash were shrouded in mystery. The world united in worship and lamentation for her on a scale not seen for decades.

First published in Zombie Jesus and Other True Stories (Dark Moon Books, 2012)

This is an idea I discussed with my brother-in-law, but it took me a long time to think up a good angle on the story. I wanted to do justice to the great ending he suggested, and turn it into something that you could imagine watching as a movie. Ultimately, a call for submissions for a 2012 anthology of alternative history stories was the catalyst that got me writing.

I'm proud of my idea for how the murders were executed – an overdose crammed into one doctored pill. One day I may re-use the idea in a locked room murder mystery. But my favourite thing about this piece is that there's not a single part you can prove to be untrue – in fact, the more you research it the more you might end up believing it.

DREADFUL PENNY

The fucking penny was trying to kill me.

I took the dreadful penny from a dead man's car. It's a 1987 penny with a little nick on the Queen's nose.

The man had come right out through the windscreen. Seven years as a paramedic and I'd never seen anything like it. He flew twenty feet and still had enough velocity when he hit the lamppost to split his head open like a watermelon.

The medical textbook says it best:

"When presented with a pulseless patient, medical professionals are required to perform CPR unless specific conditions are met which allow them to pronounce the patient as deceased. For example:

"Decapitation, incineration, severed body, and other injuries not compatible with life. If a patient is presenting with any of these conditions, it should be intuitively obvious that the patient is non-viable."

I grabbed a body bag from the ambulance.

On the way back I did a visual sweep of the car in case someone else was in there, and a glint caught my eye. Instinctively, I put my hand through the bent metal and picked up the penny from the driver's seat.

I pocketed it and went over to scoop pieces of brain into the body bag. Definitely non-viable.

On my way home that night I thought about the dead guy. I couldn't get him out of my head. I went into the Londis on Borough High Street to buy a sandwich for supper but all the fillings looked like mashed brains. I bought a plasticky salad.

I bought a Lottery scratch card too. I never win more than a couple of quid, and always end up using it to buy more scratch cards, but it keeps me dreaming. I pulled the penny out of my pocket and scratched off the silver coating right there on the counter.

It took me a few seconds to register how much I'd won. I checked three times to be sure. The man behind the counter leaned over to see what I was looking at; I jerked the ticket away and left in a hurry.

I stuffed the ticket into my pocket and left my hand there so I could feel it. I was sure everyone was looking at me. I was suddenly paranoid that I'd be attacked. I quick-marched to the Tube station.

In my other hand, I was still holding the penny. I looked at it and realised it was the one from the dead man's car.

When I got to the platform I pulled the ticket out again to check I wasn't dreaming. £250,000 . . . £250,000 . . . £250,000. I folded it back into my pocket, and dropped the penny by mistake.

The penny rolled along the platform and I chased it, trying to stamp on it. Forgive me for being a little superstitious but with a job like mine it helps to believe in higher powers. That penny had to be the luckiest penny in the world and I was not going to let it go.

I dived to catch it. I hadn't seen the incoming train. It missed my head by an inch – I think it touched my hair. I got up and dusted myself off, my heart in my mouth. After a few seconds I became dimly aware that the platform attendant was shouting at me. I ignored him and boarded the train.

I felt a bit sick by the time I got home. I think it was the adrenalin. I was convinced that I would have a heart attack or a piano would fall on my head before I managed to cash in this ticket. But I got home without being dead.

My hands were shaking, so I put the kettle on. I pulled out the ticket – the penny flicked out too and landed somewhere with a clink. I looked around my feet and on the countertop but I couldn't see it. Never mind, I thought, it can't have gone far.

I stared at the scratch card again. A quarter of a million pounds. I read all the rules and Ts & Cs on the back, and I re-checked the numbers. It seemed real. It was real. I pocketed it again. I wasn't going to let it leave my side.

The kettle boiled and I poured myself a mug of tea. I sat down and started scheming about what I would do with the money. I would buy a car. And a house. I wouldn't tell anyone, but I'd arrange mysterious windfalls for my friends and family. I wouldn't quit my job, but I'd do fewer hours.

I downed the last bit of tea and started to choke. The penny. It had fallen into the mug, and now it was in my throat. Choking is a horrible feeling. It's not that I couldn't breathe, but it was like breathing through a thin straw, and when I breathed in it felt like I was sucking the coin deeper. It hurt. It felt like a cheese grater against my larynx. I could picture the soft, fragile tube being slashed irreparably and I started to panic.

I swallowed and sucked and tried to cough. My breath started to gurgle and it became harder to suck in air. The hypoxaemia was setting in. Then I had a moment of clarity, and I scrambled around to the back of the chair. I put my diaphragm against the wooden slat and Heimliched myself so hard I think I broke a rib.

Needless to say, it worked, or I wouldn't be telling you this story.

I spat out the bloody coin and immediately vomited onto the floor. I gingerly made my way to the sink to get some water (although I did not welcome the prospect of drinking with my throat in so much pain). But the penny had got stuck between two floorboards and my shuffling feet caught it; I tripped and, in my weakened state, lost my balance and fell, cracking my head on the corner of the kitchen table.

I might have been unconscious for a while. I was aware of being on the floor, in serious pain pretty much all over my body. The fucking penny was trying to kill me.

I scraped myself off the floor, snatched the penny up and threw it out of the window. About ten seconds later, my doorbell started ringing incessantly. Muddy-headed, I stumbled to the front door and opened it.

"Did you throw this fucking penny at me?"

The man at the door had shoulders like the Hoover Dam. His right eyelid flickered as if his body was just on the edge of being in control. I opened my mouth to explain myself, and coughed a fine spray of blood all over his face. He looked even more surprised than I was.

He frantically wiped his face with his T-shirt and then started hitting me again and again, screaming, "It's in my eye! It's in my eye! You could've given me AIDS!"

He left a couple of minutes before the police arrived. My next-door neighbour called them I think. I was lying on the floor, bleeding.

"Sir?"

I muttered something. I was barely conscious.

"Oh hey," said the policeman. "You're a paramedic aren't you? I saw you earlier today, at that accident over by London Bridge. That guy who went clear through his windscreen. You know, they reckon he was wearing his seat belt, but it failed because there was something stuck in it. A coin or something."

"The penny!" I said, throat rattling. I frisked my pockets. The scratch card. That thug who had beaten me up had taken the scratch card. "He stole it! He stole it!"

"Hey, hey, calm down. You need some medical attention. Who cares about a stupid penny?"

"No, he stole –"

"Look, here's a lucky penny for you," he said, picking the penny up off the floor. "Have this one instead."

I'm in hospital now. I still have the penny. So if I die, you know why. And if you ever find yourself in possession of a 1987 penny with a little nick on the Queen's nose, get rid of it. For God's sake get rid of it.

First published in Dark Moon Digest Issue 4 (Dark Moon Books, 2011)

In 2009, a friend of mine – a creative force of nature – sent me an email about a new project. A printed journal, 3,000 copies per issue, distributed for free. This was the brief:

"The paper is called 'The London Dreadful'. It's taking inspiration from the Victorian Penny Dreadfuls, which were full of pulp melodramatic fiction for the masses. Crude storylines with an underlying tone of sex, death, and adventure. We're taking that, and updating it."

I was inspired to write Dreadful Penny for his first issue.

GONZALO HERMENEGILDO

*"I vow to fight this country," spat
Hermenegildo. "I will avenge."*

I t was a late spring day in 1981. Ana Severino
clocked off early from the paediatrics ward in
Hospital de Madrid. The new national healthcare
system meant there were more and more staff on the
ward, so no-one would notice her leave a few minutes
before the end of her shift.

She walked briskly down the busy streets. The air was
buzzing with people preparing for the fiesta. Intriguing
splashes of colour caught the corner of her eye; red
and gold streamers being cut for the floats, feathers
being dyed blue and green. She stopped to buy food
from a mercadillo. The burgeoning sun accentuated
the sweet pungent smell of meat fat sizzling on a hot
surface, the faint scent of cheeses, somewhere the
aroma of warm fresh bread, a drift of cut herbs and
roasting vegetables.

She haggled harder than usual; she had been short
of money lately, and she wanted to buy a present for
her son Juan. She bought fruits and vegetables, fish,
olive oil and a bottle of wine. Only the essentials. She

politely declined when a passing policeman offered to help carry her bags. She was looking forward to making lunch for Juan. It was his eighth birthday.

*

Two months earlier, on the twenty-third of February, Lieutenant Colonel Gonzalo Hermenegildo had attempted to overthrow the Spanish government. He stormed the Cortes with an army of two-hundred members of the paramilitary Civil Guard. They fired automatic weapons into the air, and took 350 Members of Parliament hostage.

On televisions across the world it looked like a surreal kind of opera. Hermenegildo was a short man with a dense triangular moustache, wearing a stern beret and a meticulous blue uniform. He marched back and forth directing the mass of people almost ceremonially. The hostages were instructed to lie down, and they did, as if choreographed. Hermenegildo was in centre stage, surrounded by the amphitheatre of parliamentary seats, spotlighted by shafts of light through the acrid dust from the bullet-ridden ceilings.

A brave or foolhardy hostage called out the name of the former Prime Minister, to show his solidarity for democracy and to snub the rebels. Several other hostages joined in, chanting. "Adolfo Suárez! Adolfo Suárez!" Adolfo Suárez himself drew back, trying timidly to hide. Hermenegildo fired a shot towards the dissenters, which landed in a burst of splintering wood. The crowd went instantly silent. He had not intended to miss.

Hermenegildo declared a state of emergency and ordered tanks onto the streets of Valencia. His junta commandeered all radio and TV broadcast frequencies to deliver a dogmatic ultimatum: "Spain thrived under General Franco's dictatorship. Democracy has failed. We embrace the absolute authority of King Carlos."

*

On the first of May, Ana Severino felt too ill to go into work. Her son was ill as well, but she was too weak to tend to him. Her neighbour Aarón got a call from the hospital; they were concerned by her absence. Aarón knocked and knocked on Ana's door, but there was no answer. Eventually, he let himself in through the window. He saw Ana and little Juanito, and immediately called for an ambulance.

Juan Severino was pronounced dead on arrival. The doctors did not tell Ana right away.

Ana was feverish and mumbling. Something about the food being poisoned. She had hosted a party, Juan's birthday party, and many people had eaten the food. The doctors contacted her family, and sure enough, they were sick too.

Within days, four family members had joined Ana in the hospital, all stricken with the same mysterious disease. The doctors wore stern faces and said things that Ana's family did not understand. Interstitial pulmonary infiltrates. Asthenia. Seborrhea.

Soon, more patients arrived with the same symptoms. One or two a day at first. Then six. Then thirty. The doctors could not cure them. The doctors could not explain their condition.

*

Lieutenant Colonel Gonzalo Hermenegildo's coup lasted just one day. King Carlos made a charismatic stand against him, announcing on national television that the democratic government must be defended. He ordered the armed forces to take all necessary measures to quell the insurgency. A coup would not be tolerated.

Hermenegildo had tried to drum up support from other army units around the country, but he had misjudged the strength or nature of their ideologies. His own army became nervous and they forced him to surrender.

The hostages were freed and the rebel Civil Guards were arrested. Hermenegildo was immediately transferred to a military prison. He was told he would be thrown into a solitary cell and left to rot. His throat was so filled with rage and shame that he looked forward to the jail cell, to get away from the judging eyes of his armed escorts – to put distance and time between him and his failed revolution.

At the prison he was stripped of his uniform. His triangular moustache was shaved. The Chief Warden laughed at him, then spat in his face. Hermenegildo remained silent, his teeth clenched, until just before he was left in his cell:

"I vow to fight this country," spat Hermenegildo. "I will avenge."

*

Ana's health slowly improved, but the number of cases of this mysterious illness was reaching epidemic proportions. Yesterday, 199 new cases were identified, today another 230. More deaths had been reported. The doctors had to ask her to leave the hospital to make room for sicker people. And, of course, they had to stop lying to her about her son.

Juan is dead. The doctor's parting words filled her so completely that she felt empty of anything else. She was empty even of tears. She did not go home. She walked across the hospital to the paediatrics ward, where she had not been to work for three weeks. Her fellow medics recognised her but said nothing.

The ward was lined with sick children. Two to a bed, and more spilling out onto the floor. Dozens of them. Fifty at least, maybe sixty. The air was thick with their fevered cries and desolate moans. This was a plague. A mass infection. What could it be? Something in the water supply? A virus? Judgment Day?

Ana felt weak. She leaned on the wall and closed her eyes. She tried to concentrate, to be rational. She calmed herself and gathered her thoughts. She vowed to find out what had killed her son. She marched to the cupboard and pulled out a spare uniform. She would not leave the hospital until the mystery was solved.

*

Hermenegildo persuaded a prison guard to carry messages to and from the outside without censoring them. The guard was sympathetic to Hermenegildo's cause, and was promised a great reward when the revolution finally succeeded.

Over several weeks, Hermenegildo remotely established a base of supporters, mostly Civil Guard members that had stayed out of jail after the failed coup. From his solitary prison cell, with surreptitiously exchanged little notes, Hermenegildo coordinated another attack.

Eventually, the Chief Warden caught the mutinous guard and the messages stopped. Hermenegildo's final instruction had been to attack the country and hold its people to ransom until the government and the King conceded power.

Sure enough, on a late spring day in 1981, the attack had started.

*

As the numbers of stricken people climbed into the thousands, and the numbers of dead into the hundreds, Ana was no closer to finding the cause of the epidemic. She had done countless tests on numerous patients. She had systematically tried every combination of drugs, but nobody responded to any kind of treatment.

She avoided listening to the radio or glimpsing the television. The general population had started to panic, and with the lack of any real progress the news stations had resorted to reporting rumours. People were afraid to leave their homes; afraid to eat or drink; afraid to breathe each other's air. The plague seemed inevitable.

Ana felt like she was losing energy, losing hope. Every muscle in her body ached, but she fought on, no longer out of determination to discover the cause but out of fear of returning home and leaving her son behind.

And, all around her, children kept dying. Each time another soul departed, she felt personally responsible. Doing everything she possibly could was not enough for the wailing mothers, the grieving fathers.

Each night before she slept on the hospital floor, she prayed. Only God could have the wrath to inflict such a plague. Only God could forgive its victims. She prayed to hear that one word, the word of forgiveness that would guide her to the cause and the cure of the epidemic.

Nearly two months after the first casualty, the youngest victim yet was delivered to Ana's ward. Sara Zoraida was just four months old. Sara's grandmother, Señora Zoraida, was hysterical with worry.

"Was it something I fed her?"

This struck a chord somewhere deep inside Ana's intuition. This baby was so far the only victim under six months old. Perhaps there was something that Grandma Zoraida had fed baby Sara that would normally only feature in the diet of older children and adults. She asked the question.

"I feed her formula," explained Señora Zoraida frantically, "from the supermarket. That's it, nothing else. I always sterilise the bottle. Sometimes I add a little oil to the bottle, for her health."

Ana thought back to what she had bought before Juan died. Fruits and vegetables, fish, olive oil, a bottle of wine. Only the essentials.

"Señora Zoraida," implored Ana, "what kind of oil do you use?"

"I bought olive oil. A five-litre bottle, unmarked. From the mercadillo outside the hospital."

Ana stood stunned. Señora Zoraida became even more agitated, but Ana did not notice. A five-litre bottle, unmarked. Ana's chin puckered. She cried – sobbed – for the first time in two months, for the loss of her son.

*

Hermenegildo overheard the prison guards talking in sensational whispers as they did their final rounds of the night. He leant against the door to hear. A plague. Thousands of people affected, and still spreading. No known cause, no known cure. The guards passed out of earshot. He paced in his cell, and then jumped in surprise when someone knocked on the door.

"Who is it?" called Hermenegildo.

"Shhh! I bring an important message from outside." It was the mutinous prison guard that had helped Hermenegildo reform his army. He was taking a great risk delivering this message. A note appeared through the small hole in the bottom of the door designed for food trays.

Suddenly, Hermenegildo heard a curse from the messenger guard and the sound of him running away. Then the unmistakeable, steady footfalls of the Chief Warden.

Hermenegildo read the note quickly. His face fell. The Chief Warden unlocked the door and burst in. Hermenegildo backed up against the wall, reading the end of the note, then he tried to stuff it into his mouth.

The Chief Warden grabbed it from him. It ripped. Hermenegildo swallowed half of it; the Chief Warden had the rest.

The Chief Warden beat Hermenegildo with a cosh and then retreated to the doorway to read his half of the note. His eyes widened. His jaw fell.

"You caused this plague?" uttered the Chief Warden in disbelief. "YOU?"

"Yes," replied Hermenegildo through a bloodied nose.

"Do you know how many people have died? How many children?"

"They will keep dying until this country is free of democracy and its corruption."

The Chief Warden glanced at the torn note again. "Which olive oil supplier did you poison?"

Hermenegildo had swallowed that secret.

"Which supplier did you poison?" repeated the Chief Warden. "Tell me so we can put a stop to this madness."

"Set me free and I will tell you."

"I will not set you free. You have become a disgusting terrorist. You are the most evil person in the world. Tell me the name of the factory."

Hermenegildo hesitated. His face twisted awkwardly. He fought to repress his emotions.

"No," said Hermenegildo firmly.

"You will stand there and let hundreds more people die, for the sake of saying one little word?"

Hermenegildo said nothing. The Chief Warden stared at him in wonder. Then left, locking the door behind him.

Alone in his cell, Hermenegildo allowed his stubbornness and pride to fall away, and he realised what burdens they had been. Each burning tear represented a regret, each sob an ounce of shame.

He beat on his cell door and called out the name of the factory, although he knew no-one would hear him. The one word that would save a thousand innocent lives. He called it out just to hear it echo in his own head.

*

Once the cause of the epidemic had been discovered, the government worked quickly to minimise its impact. Public service announcements were broadcast on every frequency, press conferences were held, and signs were put up at every stall in the mercadillos. An oil recall program was initiated, and free safe olive oil was made available for anyone that was concerned about their own supply.

Ana Severino was instrumental in finding the source of the outbreak. The unmarked five-litre bottles were traced back to a particular oil distributor. Their factory was immediately shut down, and the chemical agent responsible for the epidemic was isolated. But the truth provided scant comfort for Ana.

The final toll was 20,000 sick, 800 dead. The government decided not to make it public that a fledgling terrorist group were responsible; the official story was that the oil distributor had been in blatant disregard of health and safety regulations.

Gonzalo Hermenegildo was found dead in his cell the morning after the Chief Warden's visit.

First published at www.literallystories2014.com

I wrote this story in 2005, in response to a challenge on an online writers' forum. The challenge was to write a story about "The Worst Person in the World". Many years later, I dug it up, and it was finally published in 2019.

The character of Gonzalo Hermenegildo was inspired by Lieutenant-Colonel Antonio Tejero, who, on 23 February 1981, led 200 armed Civil Guard officers into the Spanish Parliament in an attempted coup d'état. King Juan Carlos I refused to endorse the coup and it ended bloodlessly, effectively spelling the end of Francoist fascism.

Later that year, a previously unknown musculoskeletal disease swept across Spain with devastating consequences. The cause was traced to the consumption of rapeseed oil that had been intended for industrial rather than food use, and tainted with aniline. Hundreds died, and thousands were left permanently disabled.

This story imagines a connection between these two incidents. But the true story behind "toxic oil syndrome" is even stranger. In reality, the lethal epidemic was nothing to do with tainted oil, but most likely caused by the consumption of toxic organophosphates used as pesticides on fruits such as tomatoes. A massive conspiracy by the Spanish government, bolstered by commercial interests, ensured the evidence was so thoroughly manipulated that the truth may never be known.

So, the surprising moral of the story is: Wash your tomatoes.

DO NOT PASS GO

If he thinks it's important to ask us, we've got to take that seriously. We've got to test him!

The doorbell chimed and my heart fluttered. I shifted my weight from foot to foot. Perhaps they had all gone out for a walk, and they wouldn't answer. It wasn't too late to turn back.

The door opened. Alice's father stood there — untidy hair, asymmetric glasses, stubble, badly fitting clothes — everything about him was chaotic, animated. He broke into a broad smile.

"Eddie! How lovely to see you!"

"Hello Mister Stride."

"What brings you out here to the boonies? Life treating you well? How's Alice?"

I didn't know which question to answer first. He stared at me expectantly, sizing me up. Moving, always moving, as if his clothes itched. A flush of warmth crawled down my spine.

"Sorry! Come in, come in, of course. Don't call me Mister Stride, that's what my research students call me."

"Thank you . . . Tom." Even with his encouragement, saying his name felt presumptuous. Which I suppose said more about me than him.

The dimly lit kitchen was full of plants; it smelled of ferns and pine. I touched a frond, which instantly curled away from me. Beyond the plants, a large lounge lit by an open fire. In the middle of the lounge was a low table surrounded by cushions, and on the cushions, two women, craning their necks towards me in a mirror of each other.

"Do we have a guest?" said one of the women, getting up.

"Ah, yes, forgot to tell you, Eddie called to say he's in the area this evening and can he drop in?" said Mr Stride, busy with the kettle.

"Hello Missus Stride," I said as the woman walked into the kitchen. Cropped hair, a gentle smile and sparkling chestnut eyes just like Alice's.

"Forgive my husband," she said. "You haven't met Julia, have you?"

I waved at Alice's sister through the ferns, and she waved tentatively back. She was maybe sixteen, gawky but blooming, almost as pretty as Alice.

"Would you like to stay for supper?" said Mrs Stride.

Mr Stride chipped in: "We were just about to start a family game of Monopoly."

"I didn't mean to interrupt," I said. "I . . . It's just that . . . Sorry. I'm a bit nervous."

"No need to be nervous here," said Mr Stride, arms wide open, "our house is yours."

I came right out with it. "I've come to ask your permission to marry Alice."

Both of them, all three of them, looked at me as if I had turned into a moose.

"I mean, um," I said, "to ask her to marry me. If that's ok."

Mrs Stride started to say something, but Mr Stride stilled her with a gesture of his hand. He stared at me; my heartbeat thudded in my skull.

Mrs Stride slapped her husband hard on the arm. "Tom, don't play with him."

"No, Pam, if he thinks it's important to ask us, we've got to take that seriously. We've got to test him!" He grinned, teeth exposed, pointing a finger up in the air. Then he hunched over for a moment, as if deep in thought, and turned to me with a wicked gleam in his eye. "Tell you what, beat us at Monopoly and you can have our blessing."

"Oh that's a spectacular idea," said Mrs Stride sarcastically, a hand against her forehead. Her expression sublimated into amused resignation. "You'll be staying for food, then."

*

Even before the game started I could see that underestimating Mr Stride would be dangerous. The first decision was which playing piece to pick, and as I looked down at the cluster of pewter tokens I realized that Mr Stride was watching me.

Julia, to my left, had chosen the car; Mrs Stride the old boot; and Mr Stride, directly across the board from me, was fondling the tiny top hat. The fire spat and crackled behind me. It smelled like Christmas.

I hovered over the Scottie dog, then the battleship, before settling on the iron. Mr Stride's expression lifted into a cunning half-smile. We put our pieces on the Go square. I hoped Alice wouldn't feel like I was gambling for her affections. No, she would understand, this wasn't a game; it was a trial.

"Roll to see who goes first," said Julia, her big eyes shining as she expertly dealt out the tiny bills to each of us.

"There'll be no mercy," said Mr Stride.

"I'll play hard," I said.

"Ha! A bit of spirit!" He rubbed his hands together like a Bond villain.

"You gonna have babies right away?" asked Julia, doling out the ones.

"Julia," scolded Mrs Stride. "They're not even married yet."

Mr Stride shot in. "And they won't get married at all if he can't prove his worth on the Monopoly board."

We played a few turns. I made small talk with Julia and Mrs Stride; Mr Stride stayed silent and watchful. I had to win the game of course, it was a matter of pride. I knew the basic tactics; stay out of jail for the first few rounds, buy up lots of property, then consolidate a set or two and start building. Easy.

"I've landed on Go," said Mr Stride, "four hundred please."

"Four hundred?" I asked. "It's two hundred."

"Yeah," said Julia, counting out the money. "But you get double when you land on the Go square."

"No you don't," I protested, frowning.

"Ha! Stride family rules!" said Mr Stride.

"Hang on," I said, waving my hands above the board, "I signed up to Parker Brothers rules."

"Not in this house. Should've thought of that before you started," he teased.

"Okay, okay, but I need to know what I'm getting myself in for."

"No kidding," smirked Julia with a sideways glance.

"So what other rules do you use?" I asked. "Free Parking?"

Mr Stride put on a pompous tone. "When you land on Free Parking you get all the tax that's been put in the middle."

"That's not how tax works!" I complained.

"And if no-one wants a property we auction it off," said Julia, "and if you roll three doubles you go to jail, and you can't collect rent when you're in jail, and —"

"That's not right either," I said, "you can collect rent in jail."

"That rule doesn't really send out the right message," explained Mrs Stride.

"Ever been in jail?" asked Mr Stride.

"Me?" I asked.

Mrs Stride hit her husband on the arm.

Mr Stride laughed. "We should know in case he wins and we have to let him marry Alice."

"I have actually," I said. All three of them stopped and looked up at me. "Well, a police cell, for busking without a licence."

"What do you play?" asked Julia.

"Harmonica. I wasn't even busking really."

"No sense of humour, some policemen," said Mr Stride, rolling the dice.

Julia's eyes were even wider than normal. "I can't believe they put you in prison for playing the harmonica!"

"You haven't heard him play, maybe he deserved it," said Mr Stride, and he braced himself for an arm-slap.

*

When I bought one of the green plastic houses he asked me where Alice and I would live. When I had to pay £50 in doctor's fees he asked me about my health. When I won second prize at a beauty contest he commented on my looks. By the time the last properties were being bought, he had interrogated me about almost everything.

I landed on Free Parking and collected a few hundred pounds from the middle, without saying a word. Mr Stride pursed his lips as if holding back a snide comment. I bought more houses, and couldn't resist a peek at Mr Stride's scant money pile.

"Don't get cocky now," he said. He moved his top hat and landed on Mayfair. He couldn't afford to buy it.

Julia conducted the auction as if she was selling cattle. "Do I hear twohundredtwohundred wehaveabidder twofifty themanintheblueshirt . . ."

I was bidding against Mr Stride. I priced him out, but he mortgaged Electric Company and bid £80 more. I mortgaged Park Lane to outbid him again. He looked annoyed.

"Look, let me have it and I'll pay for the wedding," he said. I think I must have flinched, because he forced a laugh and said quickly, "assuming you win my permission to marry at all, of course."

There was a momentary silence during which I tried not to make eye contact with Mr Stride.

"I bid five hundred pounds," said Mrs Stride.

"Sold!" said Julia, banking Mrs Stride's money with admirable speed. She rolled the dice and tried to pretend that there had been no awkward moment.

On my next turn I traded with Mrs Stride to complete the red set. I was doing ok, but I felt tense, as if a spring was coiled inside my belly.

"That's not fair," said Mr Stride. "You gave him an easy trade. You want him to win."

"We got a set each. It's —" I cut myself short before I said anything stupid.

Mr Stride growled. "You'll be sore when you lose and you can't marry Alice. It'll be such a tragedy."

I stayed quiet, fiddling with one of my orange property cards.

He snorted and rolled a double one. Chance: "Make general repairs on all your property." When he saw how many houses he would have to sell, he leapt up and looked like he might flip the table.

"Tom, sit down," ordered Mrs Stride.

"He's an even worse winner," whispered Julia in my direction.

Grumbling, he settled his debt and rolled again. As he moved his token, I could see where he was going to end up. Vine Street, my star property, with three houses. My back went clammy.

"That's terrible luck," said Mrs Stride.

"That's six hundred pounds," said Julia. "You're bankrupt."

Mr Stride slapped the table hard, scattering the pieces, and stormed out of the room. There was a lingering silence, the three remaining players not sure where to look.

With a tight smile, Mrs Stride said, "Still want to marry Alice?"

At the mention of her name, my heart swelled with longing. I nodded.

Her shoulders relaxed. "Then, Eddie, I donate all my assets to you. Julia?"

Julia's wide eyes flicked back and forth. "What? Oh . . . yeah," she said, and gave me her stack of bills too.

Mrs Stride grinned. "Anyone who can survive a Stride family game of Monopoly is certainly worthy of Alice."

Mr Stride marched back in. He paced for a moment, then his eyes sparked with mischief. He clapped a hand on Julia's shoulders, puffed up his chest and said, "Double or nothing!"

First published at www.dimeshowreview.com

Board games have always been an obsession for me. At the time of writing, I have about 150 board and card games in my collection. Monopoly isn't one of them, but I still have a soft spot for it, in all its obnoxious glory.

I think many people have stories about fighting over Monopoly as a family – knowing it is a uniquely exasperating torture, but playing anyway. I wanted to capture some of that in this story.

I'm not sure when I wrote this story, sometime in the early 2010s, but the first draft didn't work at all. Eventually, I reworked it, and it was published in 2017.

SECOND PLACE

> *I sat on the filthy pavement across from her. Just sat, and waited for her to forgive me.*

"Good evening, Mr Citrone, please sit down." The man sat on the other side of the desk was dressed in a suit so sharp it could cut a diamond. This was Robin Murgatroyd – *the* Robin Murgatroyd – agitator, seer, demigod. He looked at me with such intensity, such authority, I don't think I could have resisted any command he gave. I want that, I thought. I want to be able to have such presence, to own a room so completely.

I sat. Studied his posture, his micro-expressions, his movements, mirroring him, learning.

"Lambert?" he said. "Am I pronouncing it correctly? Or is it Lam-*bear*?"

"The French way. My parents are French."

"Your CV is impressive. You won the Banker last year. Yours was the second highest investment banking portfolio performance in Europe."

"Yes."

He waved his hand dismissively. "Second best. We only employ the best."

"You employ connections. You employ routes to industry. You employ people who can make money. I can make money."

He nodded. "So you're smart. Why not stay in investment banking? Why go into VC?"

"Because investment banking is too conservative."

Murgatroyd laughed. A hearty laugh, full and free. I wasn't sure if he was mocking me. But he wouldn't dismiss me. The fact that he was seeing me at all meant he was interested. I'd cracked the first layer of his façade, now I just needed to navigate the fault line.

A smile remained on his lips. "Your breakthrough investment was Freightshare, right? Selling it to Amazon was a coup, I'll grant you that."

"I'm no one-hit wonder. We're heading into a new economy of common property. I'm on the inside with a couple of start-ups that –"

"Ok, ok, you've convinced me. Almost."

I felt a surge of adrenalin. The home stretch. I could taste victory. Control. Concentrate.

Murgatroyd leaned forward. "Tell me. What's your weakness?"

"I cannot stand being second place."

"Second place." Murgatroyd smirked. "You'd better get used to it if you want to work with us."

"What do you mean?"

"You haven't met Sadie Carmine."

*

Working for Murgatroyd was relentless. It was a small team, only fourteen partners and about fifty so-called principals with a limited investment portfolio. I started as a principal, on a six-month probation, with £5 million to spend and no vote on the board.

I worked my butt off, schmoozing with anyone I could get access to in the day, researching and reading late into the night. There was an office, which I used occasionally, but there was so much angst between the partners it was a pretty toxic environment. Every week Murgatroyd called a team meeting and fired one of us. Often the principals didn't last more than a couple of months. Occasionally a new batch would come in. We were like a bunch of teenage girls in a catfight over the affections of Robin Murgatroyd.

In the middle of the office was a white porcelain bowl, which was always kept stocked with what looked like breath mints. But they weren't breath mints, they were some kind of amphetamine. I never partook, but it bothered me that they were so brazenly out in the open. It was like a statement, that we were better than the petty rules and regulations that governed the outside world. Distasteful.

The breath mints were popular with most of the employees, though. None more so than the intriguing Sadie Carmine. She took handfuls of them like candy. I watched her closely. Murgatroyd had said she was the best, so naturally she was the one to beat.

But I couldn't understand it. She was a partner, of course, but she seemed to treat work like a joke. She would turn up an hour late for board meetings. She would dance through the office flirting with the data monkeys as if she was drunk, wearing last night's evening gown with her hair mussed up like she'd just got out of bed.

She got away with it, somehow. Or, rather, she didn't just get away with it, she exuded a kind of pied piper magnetism that made you feel like you should be behaving the same way. Like you were taking life too seriously and should lighten up. There was something magic about her.

Almost from the first day, she noticed I was paying attention to her. I mean, all the heterosexual men she came within ten metres of paid her attention, but I was taking notes. She teased me. Not directly, but every time she saw me she made a show of coming over and speaking to the person sitting next to me. Or she watched me watching her from across the room, waiting until I lost the game of chicken and looked away.

From what I could gather, she was into energy. Graphene batteries, solar cells, wearable kinetics, remote power. But then I'd see her having some deeply technical conversation about the manufacturing processes of synthetic oil, or the stochastics of forex arbitrage, or the long-term prospects of the pod hotel industry. Basically she seemed to know everything.

Meanwhile, I put my £5 million into a kind of executive lifestyle rental company – they were targeting wealthy young jetsetters whose main residence was usually in a desirable city centre, and usually empty. Airbnb for people too rich and busy to condescend to using Airbnb.

Putting all my portfolio money into one company was a gamble, but I was looking for a short-term win. I wanted to prove my worth irrefutably before my probation was up. I reckoned I could get the app completed and sold for triple the money within four months. I did it in three.

I was constantly exhausted. Exhilarated. And, increasingly, as I learned more about Sadie Carmine, enthralled. It took me the full six months to muster the courage to ask her if she wanted to join me for a drink. I didn't want to ask until I was sure she'd say yes.

*

She took me to a pub on a council estate. From the outside it looked like the kind of place British National Party members could talk shop with white supremacists. I figured she was trying to set me on edge, keep me on my toes. But inside the place was surprising. A kind of hipster heaven, with retro memorabilia glued to every surface, bearded graphic designers getting passionate about David McCandless, and twelve craft beers on tap.

We sat in a quiet corner and ordered halloumi burgers.

"How did you discover this place?" I asked. We were drinking Cokes, but hers had two shots of rum.

"One of my boyfriends. Film student. I like that this place is full of arty types; I find it charming."

"You're about as far from an arty type as I've ever seen."

She pouted. "I went to art school. The Royal Academy."

"Really?"

"Yeah, for six months. Wasn't really a student there, I just showed up at lectures. I submitted a piece for the final exhibition. They were impressed, until they figured out I wasn't supposed to be there."

"You are something else."

Sadie smiled. She finished her rum and coke and signalled to the bar staff to bring two more.

"I don't drink," I said.

"I don't hang out with men who take themselves so seriously."

Our food arrived, and the drinks shortly after. She clinked my glass. Hesitantly, I drank. We made small talk while we ate. I nervously sipped at the rum and coke until it was all gone, but then another appeared in its place.

"Tell me your story," I said, feeling bolder.

"Most boring story in the world."

"Tell it."

"Only child. Born in Stoke-on-Trent to parents that wanted a boy. Dad ran his own factory making tiny plastic bits on contract for Land Rover. He was pretty mad when he realised I had no interest in taking over from him. I played truant at school a lot, read voraciously, ran away to London when I was sixteen.

Been drifting from job to job ever since. You know, the usual."

"You are like no one I've ever met."

"You, however, Monsieur Citrone, are entirely predictable."

"What do you mean?"

"You were born to wealthy French landowners. A middle child. Brought up with discipline and privilege, and a huge chip on your shoulder. Studied law at Oxford because your daddy did, topped it up with an FCA. You got in with a bunch of wannabe Warren Buffets, made some lucky calls, and now you're on the fast track to become partner in the most prestigious VC firm in Europe."

"I studied at Cambridge."

"Same diff."

"You Googled me."

Sadie shrugged and smiled coyly.

"Were you really born in Stoke-on-Trent?" I asked.

"One of the benefits of being a committed nihilist is I have no reason to lie. I don't think I've lied since I was four. It doesn't suit me."

"How did you end up in venture capital?"

"I cheated."

"What? Did you sleep with Murgatroyd?"

"Give me more credit. I fuck a lot of men, but not men like him."

"He's a god."

"He's a crook."

"I don't buy it. You woke up one day and decided to weasel your way into being a partner at a leading VC firm? What really made you want to do this?"

"Someone said I couldn't."

I leant back in my chair. I'd lost track of whether this was my third rum and coke or my fourth – and she seemed to be drinking two for every one of mine. My brain dilated from the alcohol, my hands started gently trembling from the caffeine. At that moment Sadie seemed to me like a column of certitude in a sea of madness. Bold and unwavering. I wanted to cling on and watch the world revolve from her steadfast perspective. "Is there anything you can't do?"

Sadie shook her head.

"I bet I can beat you at something." I looked around the bar, hunting for inspiration. I found a tatty old chess board in a stack of 80s kids' games. "I was Vichy chess champion in my teenage years."

"OK," said Sadie, sizing me up. "If you win, I get to fuck you. If not, I fuck that guy." She pointed to a stubble-faced young beatnik sitting at the far end of the bar typing on a Chromebook.

"Who's he?"

"Don't know."

So we played. She took white. She made thoughtless, infuriating moves that messed with my opening strategies, but I couldn't see how to refute them. After a couple of exchanges she was down on material, and I was battling against the fog of drunkenness to focus on finishing her off. She played so damn *fast*, and even though she showed no signs of impatience I felt like I had to play fast too.

I ended up with a king and a knight against her king. A stalemate position. She shrugged her shoulders and went to chat up the beatnik, leaving me with the dregs of my last rum and coke. I don't know what she said to him, but it must have been pretty blunt, because within two minutes they'd left together.

The fire in my belly crackled and roared.

*

It took me nine more months to make partner. I thought about Sadie a lot during that time. Relished every opportunity to spend time with her. She was playful with me, indulged my attention, but never opened up. I longed to understand her, but she remained a tantalising mystery. A puzzle that resisted my most determined efforts to solve.

I never slept with her, as much as I wanted to. She used her sexuality to manipulate anyone that wasn't sufficiently intimidated by her frightening intellect – but I wanted to stay on even terms.

By the time I finally made it into the boardroom, I was second place in the performance rankings. Guess who was in the number one slot. It was galling how little effort it seemed to take her to stay on top.

I accompanied her out of work a few times. Inevitably, she would go to a bar or nightclub to get high, involve herself in ridiculous political debates with drunken young men, and end up taking one of them to the toilets for a more intimate encounter. It hurt to watch her debase herself like that, but sometimes I got the impression she was more aware of me than she let on, and she was doing it to tease me.

Once, just once, I saw beyond her façade. On the way to a client one morning, I went to the city library to look up some obscure piece of tax law. I wouldn't have noticed her, except that she ran away when she saw me. She'd been pretending to read a book, but I could swear she'd been crying. I called her name, looked for her, but she was gone. When I asked her about it later, she changed the subject.

Her behaviour at work, never conventional in the first place, became increasingly erratic. Most days she wasn't turning up at all, and when she did she'd have a black eye, or she'd fall asleep in the board meeting and wake up with a random outburst, or she'd vomit in the rubber tree pot.

When she came in and saw that she'd dropped from first to seventh on the performance rankings, she turned and left without a word. We never saw in her the office again. Seeing my name at the top of the rankings at last should have been cause for celebration, but it was a hollow victory.

I was still working my butt off for Murgatroyd, but I couldn't let Sadie go. In the snatches of spare time I had, I scoured the city for her. I searched the bars, the clubs, the libraries. I looked for someone who had known her at the Royal College of Art, and all the other crazy places she said she'd worked or studied.

I got her address from Murgatroyd's secretary, but she wasn't living there anymore.

My work suffered. I wanted to do well, but I wanted even more to find Sadie. I tracked down her parents. There aren't many Carmines living in Stoke-on-Trent. They were angry, said she was a hopeless drug addict and she'd stolen from them. She was wanted by the police in two cities. They had no idea where she was and didn't care anymore.

I started searching the morgues.

After weeks of this, hope had all but burned out. And, then, when I'd almost given up, there she was. In an alley, huddled in a covered nook with a whacked out junkie asleep on her lap.

She was barely recognisable, wearing men's clothes that were tatty and stained, her skin patchy and wan, her hair cut short. She looked up at me with dull eyes. Her beauty still radiated from behind the mask of wretchedness.

"Sadie," I said.

She looked away, saying nothing. I knelt down and offered her the bottle of mineral water I was holding. She took it and drank it all.

"Sadie?"

"Go away. I don't need you, I'm fine," she said through cracked lips. My heart beat in my throat.

"You can't tell me you're happy here."

"I'm no less happy than I've ever been."

I saw then that she spoke the truth. The puzzle pieces started falling into place. She had never been happy. She was scared. I thought about how hard she'd had to fight to prove herself against the men in her life constantly trying to exploit her or put her down. And by trying to better her, I'd been one of them. My cheeks prickled with shame.

"I love you Sadie. I'm sorry I never told you that before. I never realised it. I've been as bad as all the others. I want to help you."

"Go away, Lambert," she said. I looked down at my feet. Nodded, trying to hide the pain that was building inside me. I took off my jacket and gave it to her. Gave her all the cash in my wallet too. She looked at me with contempt, but she took it.

I wanted to give her more. To talk with her. To ask her where I could see her again. To tell her where to find me. But it all felt futile. I turned to leave, but I couldn't bear to.

"You weren't as bad as all the others," she said. My heart fluttered. I sensed a crack of hope return. The impossible suddenly seemed worth a try. Maybe even if it cost everything.

I sat on the filthy pavement across from her. Just sat, and waited for her to forgive me.

*

It was a difficult time. But I'd never been surer that I was doing the right thing. Back when my life was all about striving to be the best, if you'd asked me why it was so important I don't think I would have been able to tell you. Surprisingly, I didn't miss that life very much.

Sadie tried to shake me off at first. She ran; I followed. She disappeared into shady clubs into which I was not allowed to enter; I waited for her. She ordered a pair of thugs to hurt me; I took the beating.

After two days I was thirsty and hungry and cold to my bones, and she took pity on me. She let me into one of the iniquitous dens that were her new home, and she tried new ways to get rid of me. She tried to shock me with her incautious drug taking and depraved sexual antics. She insulted me to her fellow junkies, saying that I was a worthless stalker. That I was obsessed with winning, and had the affront to think I could win her, as if she was a lifeless chattel. I hated myself then, but I persisted.

Finally, she agreed to come back to my place. She ate everything in my fridge and fell asleep on the sofa. I spent an hour in the shower before I felt clean again. I threw out the stinking suit I'd been wearing for days, laid out clothes for her, and went to bed.

In the morning I felt refreshed and ravenously hungry. Sadie still slept, looking half-dead. I went out to buy food. Stopped by the office on the way to confirm what I suspected: that I'd been fired in my absence. Never mind, I thought, I had more than enough money to get by for a while.

When I returned, laden with supermarket shopping bags, my flat had been trashed. She had stolen money, clothes, even my passport. I ate my breakfast among the ruins, and then set out to find her again.

I knew her regular haunts by then, but I didn't expect to find her as easily as I did. It frightened me; if she was still just trying to put me off she'd have gone into hiding again, but no – this time she'd really lost control.

She was lost in a heroin haze, conscious but unaware of her surroundings. I picked up her stick-like frame and carried her all the way back to the flat. I threw away her clothes, bathed her, gave her food and water, and then called for help. We took a taxi to a rehab clinic in Surrey, and by the time she was coming round she was signed up for a six-week residential treatment plan.

I spent a few hours with her every day. After the first week, I stopped going home. We slept next to each other in her queen bed in the clinic. She clung on to me like a startled child. My heart swelled and enveloped her, and at last, she took me in.

When the six weeks was up she turned herself in to the police. She was given an eight month suspended sentence, conditional on staying clean and sober. She moved in with me and made the place her own.

It was soon clear we both needed to find jobs again. She needed a period of routine and stability, something to keep herself occupied and intellectually stimulated. And I needed to get back into the game – not to mention the fact that money was running low.

So I went begging back to Murgatroyd. Despite my insistence that she stay away, Sadie came with me. Once again, I found myself in Murgatroyd's office, adrenalin pumping, facing down his searing gaze.

"Mr Citrone, Miss Carmine, please have a seat," he said.

"Mr Murgatroyd," I said, "I'll level with you. I'd like my job back."

"Certainly not." The three of us sat in silence for a moment. "Did you have anything else you wanted to ask me, or can I get on with my day?"

"I was your number one performer. Start me as a principal again if you have to."

"Is Sadie asking for a job too?"

Sadie shook her head and spoke. "You need him, Murgatroyd. He can walk into any VC job in the world right now, and he'll make so much money people will start talking about him instead of you."

"The answer is no." Murgatroyd addressed me. "I need people who are willing to put everything else aside to succeed. But now you've gone and fallen for this jailbird, and you've already proven you'll put her before this company. You'll want to spend time with her, soon you'll want to start a family. I don't need that."

Murgatroyd turned to Sadie. "You're different. Being distracted doesn't seem to hold you back. But without guzzling speed by the fistful to enable your prodigiously carnal networking methods and your all-night library sessions, I don't think you'll be able to keep up."

Sadie smiled. "You're still as charming as ever, Murgatroyd."

"As are you. I can offer you a job as personal assistant, at half your previous salary. Take it or leave."

Sadie leant back, folded her arms across her chest.

"You aren't seriously considering this?" I asked. "This is a toxic environment. He's poison."

She nodded at Murgatroyd. "I'll take your crummy job."

As soon as we had left the office, I chastised Sadie. "Are you insane?"

She shrugged. "It'll buy us time for you to get back on your feet."

"I don't buy it. What really made you accept that job?"

She looked me in the eye. "You told me I shouldn't."

I stopped in my tracks. I knew then that she was bigger than me, and always would be. My stomach churned with a terrible cocktail of selfless love and anxious self-doubt, swirling against each other and refusing to reconcile, like oil and water.

All my life, I wanted to be the best. I needed to be in control. But this woman – this reckless, broken, infuriating tramp-savant – had turned my world upside-down. I loved her so hard it felt like fear, and it was at that moment I finally realised what that meant. Maybe love was always this way and I'd been too self-centred to notice:

To be with her, I would always have to come in second place.

Written in 2015, this was not initially intended as a short story, but as a character study for the protagonists of a feature film I was writing. The film, which tells the story of Sadie and Lambert's encounter with the Devil, never (yet?) made it into production.

THE MAN WHO MARRIED HIMSELF

*Will you keep yourself as a husband, to
live as one in marriage?*

"Why not?"

With those two words, my good friend
Reverend Zatarga changed the course of
my life. When he said them to me, he had just spent two
hours on the telephone with Bishop Fleming discussing
various sections of the Bible in excruciatingly fine
detail. He pointed out that Leviticus warns Christians
not to marry their sister, aunt, mother, mother-in-
law, daughter or even their granddaughter (should
they be tempted). But nowhere in the Good Book is
there a rule against marrying oneself. So when I told
Reverend Zatarga that was exactly what I wanted to
do, he eventually conceded those two fateful words:

"Why not?"

Of course, the Bible also neglects to forbid anyone
from marrying great-grandmothers, tables or pet fish.
I wouldn't be surprised to learn that Bishop Fleming
ended up marrying his beloved French poodle as a
result of all this. Or his blanket – after all, he's been
sleeping with it for years. Anyway, once I convinced

the good Reverend to let me marry the man of my dreams, I had to convince my mother and father. I'd have to say that between an international religion, firmly established for two millennia, and my own humble parents – my parents were far more difficult to persuade.

My mother just wouldn't take it seriously at first. OK, very few people took it seriously, but I needed her to know I meant it. She kept asking me silly things like, "Why marry? You can just live with yourself," or, "What will you wear for the wedding?"

And sadly, it drove my father quite mad. Literally. For years after the wedding he spent days typing up articles for a wide variety of news journals, record books and space administration newsletters claiming that he was the first person to have had sex in space. He seemed quite convinced, despite the fact that the closest he had come to space was the big button on his computer keyboard. When asked who he had allegedly had sex with, he would usually pause briefly for dramatic effect, turn his wild eyes towards you and yell shrilly: "Myself!"

I would have hoped that I could trust my best friends to be sympathetic towards my cause, but I think it was all a bit of a joke for them. They were often supportive, but since the wedding they just spend a lot of time making fun of me. Some of the wedding presents I received from them were quite demeaning: pornographic magazines, silk gloves – even a ceiling mirror. And I'm disappointed in them for not stifling their mirth when Reverend Zatarga recited the marriage vows: "Will you keep yourself as a husband, to live as one in marriage? Will you love and comfort yourself, obey and honour yourself in sickness and in health, and be faithful to yourself as long as you shall live?" I swear one of my friends wet himself laughing.

I had a great honeymoon in Las Vegas, gambling away all my savings with nobody to nag me about how much money I was spending. I had a penthouse suite in the Luxor hotel for the night of consummation . . .

I had many reasons for getting married when I did, apart from the tax benefits of course (trying to make the tax inspector understand that I was my own spouse was hell, though). Ever since I understood the concept of wedlock, I longed for a partner that I could trust. I wanted to have someone with me always, to whom I could tell all my deepest, darkest secrets without having them laugh at me. Unfortunately, although getting girlfriends was usually not too big a problem for me, I tended to have horribly bad taste. Then I realised that my perfect partner was closer to home than anyone could have guessed.

Altogether, I think the marriage was a great success for the most part. I rarely argued with my spouse – in fact, I found myself to be the best conversation holder around. The few times that I did argue, I always won. And the sex was – well, it was whatever I made of it.

There was some media intrusion of course, lots of cheap journalists trying to cash in on this unusual union. I found some of their articles amusing, and others quite offensive, especially the ones dubbing me the most conceited and/or narcissistic man in the world. I don't think I'm such an egotist, I just happen to enjoy my own company.

I suppose it was a hormonal thing, a stage of life or something, that made me suddenly crave a child. The cliché is that I realised I was mortal, and I therefore wanted to pass on my genes. So after many days weighing up the pros and cons I decided to split up from my husband in order to find a wife. I had a chat with Reverend Zatarga, and he informed me that I couldn't just file for a divorce at a moment's notice. I had to have legitimate justification. Curiously, wanting a baby wasn't on the list of valid reasons to divorce.

As the good Reverend explained, I could only divorce if I had been living apart from my spouse for at least a year – which would be difficult without major surgery – or if my spouse had treated me cruelly or been imprisoned for at least a year . . . I wasn't particularly willing to beat myself up a bit or lounge around in prison just so I could divorce myself. That left one option: Adultery. I just had to have sex with someone other than myself; normal, straight, human sex and I could be free from the bonds of marriage.

And so it was that I reluctantly removed my wedding ring and started searching for a mate. My friends were mean about it, saying that I was separating to stop myself from going blind. I think my mother was relieved when I told her that my relationship with myself was coming to an end. My father just paused for dramatic effect, turned his wild eyes towards me and yelled shrilly: "Myself!" Maybe he really is on another world.

I expected it to take me quite a while to find someone who was both willing to sleep with me and who hadn't read the newspapers enough to know that I was already married, but I soon found a plain-faced Malaysian girl who was relatively easy to seduce. The sex was, to be honest, rather disappointing. It seemed that she knew almost nothing of what turns a man on, whereas by that point I myself had become quite an expert. I suppose it wasn't great for her either – I wasn't practised in pleasuring members of the fairer sex.

The divorce was easy after that. It seemed that the church was keen to split me apart, as if my marriage had been a big mistake. I felt quite lonely for several months after the break-up. At least the local psychiatrist (specialising in multiple-personality disorders) stopped sending me his damned business cards every week.

It took me nearly a decade to find a good wife who didn't think she'd be marrying into a threesome. Most of that time was just waiting for the media to forget about "The Man Who Married Himself". Meanwhile, I wrote an autobiography with that very title. Included in the book was a detailed account of my marriage to myself, including the ups and downs of living with myself, how I dealt with everyone's criticism of me and my husband, and some intimate details of my relationship. I think it was these sections that made the book a real success when it was published some years later. People were curious to read about the implications of such an unusual marriage. I suppose it made people think. They would read my book and ask themselves: "Am I easy to live with? If I had to live with me, could I do it?" They all stopped searching for their Mister or Little Miss Right for just a moment to ask themselves if *they* would ever make a good spouse – for *anyone*.

I didn't hear of any copycat self-marriages, which probably means either the media lost interest or the church is determined not to let it happen again. Anyway, that's all behind me now. My wife and I have just moved into a new home, big enough to accommodate our new child when he is born. I am happy now. In fact, right now I can't wipe the smile off my face – you see, our next-door neighbours are Bishop Fleming and his lovely wife, the French poodle.

First published at www.eastoftheweb.com

I wrote this story way back in 1999. Since then, I've heard of quite a few people marrying themselves – every time another case gets reported my friends and family forward me the news article.

In 2010 an award-winning short film adaptation was released, which I co-wrote. The film starred Richard E Grant, Celia Imrie, Emilia Fox and Warren Clarke. I was lucky enough to meet some of the cast. One piece of advice given to me by Warren Clarke has always stuck with me:

"Write bigger."

CORA

Did you know that there are more people alive today than have died since the dawn of history?

I realised I was the last person awake, apart from the hosts, so I prepared to leave. They weren't having any of it – they gave me a couple of sofa cushions and insisted that I crash in the spare room, if I could find any floor space.

I got up and wove my way through the debris from the house party. The hosts showed me the way and bid me goodnight. As I climbed the stairs, the light dimmed until I was feeling my way along the walls.

I stepped over bodies asleep on the landing. I nearly toppled twice, my balance compromised by holding the bulky sofa cushions. I felt my way to the spare-room door, and groped around in vain for a light switch.

Giving up, I swept my foot along the floor like a metal detector, trying to find an empty space in the pitch blackness. But there were people sleeping here too.

My thigh brushed against something – a bed. I abandoned the sofa cushions at the foot of someone in a sleeping bag, who was sufficiently drunk and unconscious not to notice.

I felt across the width of the bed. When my hands hit nothing, I became bolder and felt further up. To my surprise, the bed seemed empty.

I climbed aboard, running my tongue over my fuzzy teeth and regretting that I would not brush them tonight. As soon as I lay down, my head gently throbbed as though my hangover was already kicking in.

Huddled on one side of the bed, I stripped down to my boxers in the dark. I ditched my clothes next to me and felt around for a pillow.

"Yeep!"

"Oh! I'm sorry," I whispered to the girl who had shrieked when my hand had landed on her bare skin. She'd been curled up in one small corner of the bed. "I didn't know you were there!"

"I wasn't." She giggled.

I cautiously reached out into the dark to find my clothes. "I'll find a space on the floor."

"Don't be so silly." She sighed languorously, stretching out so that an arm and a leg pinned me back to the bed. "This is a *biiiiiig* bed. We can share it."

She rolled away from me. It crossed my mind that she had probably just pushed my clothes off the bed onto some unsuspecting drunkard sleeping on the floor.

"I do move around a lot though," she said. "Pardon me if I disturb you." She shuffled somewhere in the dark.

"I'll be fine, I'm a heavy sleeper."

"Pity. I'm an insomniac."

There was a moment of silence. I felt like we were the last two people awake for miles.

She squirmed, prodding my shoulder. "Did you know that there are more people alive today than have died since the dawn of history?" she said, out of nowhere.

I thought about it. "That can't be."

"It's true. The population of the world has increased so dramatically over the last hundred years, and all those people are still alive. There are six billion people alive right now, and it hasn't been that long since there were only a few hundred thousand people on the whole planet."

I imagined her gesticulating, drawing a steep exponential curve in the air. I didn't believe her. "But humans have been around for a hundred and fifty thousand years. Even if –"

"Ah, that's the catch," she interrupted. "It's only since the dawn of history."

"When did history start?"

"With writing. Say, five thousand years ago."

"So fewer people have died in the last five thousand years than are alive today?"

"Makes you feel small, doesn't it?" she said, and shuffled again. "Oh, do you want a pillow? I'm hogging them all."

"Oof!" I exhaled as a pillow landed on my midriff. "Are you trying to start a pillow fight?"

"I don't need it. It's just that I hug the pillows sometimes when I'm trying to sleep."

"What's your name?"

She told me and I forgot it instantly. I remember it as Cora, but that's a guess. I know my memory of the night is faulty because I can almost recall how she looked, but I never saw her.

She didn't ask me my name. She asked me what I did for a living.

"I'm doing admin for local government," I answered.

"What do you really want to do?"

"Well, I want to be a writer. One day. But that's not going to make me a living, at least not yet. So I have to do a job."

"But you know what you want to do. That's amazing."

"Yeah. Although sometimes I feel like I'm deluding myself. If I want to write I should be writing, not doing dead-end admin."

"I know how you feel," she confided, shifting again. I could hear from her voice that she was facing me directly now. "I'm living a dead-end life."

"What do you mean?"

"I have no idea what I want to do. So I'm doing a menial job because it's easy. I'm just killing time until . . ." She paused.

"Until what?"

132

"Exactly. Until what. It's depressing."

I felt a wave of drunkenness wash over me. My eyes saw dancing patterns in the black. "How old are you?" I asked.

"Twenty-three."

"So you've only been an adult for five years. You've only been able to make your own decisions about your life for five years. Think how long that's been – and you have maybe a dozen of those five-year stints left. That's a dozen more lifetimes you can have. So don't give up yet."

She sighed. "It's too much, though. Too difficult. How do I decide what to do with the next five years, let alone my life?"

"Do whatever you want."

"I don't know what I want. There are too many options. Meanwhile, I'm coasting along the path of least resistance. I don't want anything badly enough to pour my heart and soul into it – I admire people who do."

"Ah, the curse of freedom," I countered with mild sarcasm.

"Exactly. We have too much freedom. It's a sickness. A hundred years ago, we'd have been allocated a job for life, and a partner for life. Our decisions were dictated by a firm moral code, religion. And ambition was defined as rising above those modest expectations."

"I see what you mean," I admitted. "When there's only one path, there's one way to succeed and one way to fail. And now we have a million ways to fail. But we also have so many more ways to succeed."

"Success is impossible when everyone has such freedom, because there's always someone out there doing it better than you. When conformity was the rule, success was easy. A hundred years ago, I just had to be a good housewife, well-mannered and devout."

"Thousands of feminists are turning in their graves right now."

"It sounds stupid, but I'm envious of people who've had some kind of tragedy in their life. If you're homeless, or you've got no legs or whatever, success is easy. Your freedom is restricted, so the path is clearer."

I frowned in the darkness. "You don't really want that, do you?"

I heard her inhale as if she was about to respond, but she said nothing. It came out as a sigh.

She reached over and tickled me. I laughed, trying to stay quiet, and reflexively slapped her arms away. It was a thrill, flirting with this stranger in the dark.

She dived for my midriff again with tickling fingers and I took her wrists and pushed them back towards her. I brushed against her breasts and snapped my hands away.

"What are you wearing?" I asked.

"Just knickers," she replied. "I've got my nightie, but it's so dark in here I took it off before you came in."

"Sorry I touched you."

"Don't worry, it was my fault."

"Are you going to sleep like that?"

"Oh, no. I'm an insomniac, I told you. I probably won't sleep at all."

She was much closer now. I could smell her skin. I moved my arm so that it was touching her, but only barely. Probably her leg. I tried to make it seem casual, as if it was the result of inadvertent restlessness in the dark, but I left it there, feeling her warmth.

"I just want to be different, you know. Unique," she murmured, more softly than before.

"Everyone's unique."

"That's the problem."

I felt tired, and let her words drift through me. A couple of times I thought I had responded, but then realised I hadn't, and I had to make a real effort to lift the conscious part of my brain into speech.

But then I felt her hand touching me, searching. I became wide awake again. I shrank away as her hand wandered close to my groin. I would be embarrassed if she touched me there, especially at that moment.

The silence became as complete as the darkness as her wandering hand persisted, and found me. My breathing deepened as she massaged me beneath my boxer shorts. I closed my eyes and imagined what she looked like.

Without stopping, she took my hand and placed it on her breast. With my other senses stifled, I quivered with the pleasure of her touch, her feminine texture.

Then I heard her gentle breathing become irregular, and I remembered that we were not alone in this room. Yet we were each more alone than ever.

She retreated for a tantalising moment and I heard the telltale sound of her knickers being slipped off. There was movement on the bed, and suddenly I was aware that she was invisibly straddling me.

"I don't have protection," I whispered.

"It's OK."

She pulled down my boxers. Some part of my brain resisted, but not strongly enough to translate into physical movement. Warm and yielding, she enveloped me. Neither of us moved at first, just savouring the sensation.

Softly, she rocked. I put my hands on her sides, feeling taut stomach muscles. I gasped as orgasm rippled through me, and into her.

Then it was as if she disappeared, as if she disengaged and left without me noticing. The bed felt empty. I must have fallen asleep.

I awoke feeling tired, as if I had not slept but been unconscious. Any hangover I deserved had passed, leaving behind only an echo of dread, as if something unexplained was wrong. Thick curtains had been pulled aside and the sun shone through the windows.

There were still some party guests sleeping haphazardly on the floor, but I was alone on the bed. I closed my eyes for a few minutes, remembering Cora. Then I got up.

I found a bathroom and splashed water on my face. I borrowed a toothbrush and cleaned my mouth out.

I dared to venture back into the bedroom to look for my clothes. As I cast my eyes about the room I looked for faces that might be hers.

Once dressed, I followed the smell of breakfast cooking downstairs and found the hosts with a smattering of guests. My recall of names and faces is unreliable at best, but when alcohol is thrown into the mix I don't even bother trying.

I made small talk and ate sausages and fried toast. My eyes absorbed every face in the room and I tried to guess. None of them gave me any signal. No naughty secrets were coaxed into mischievous smiles on my account.

But she wouldn't have known who I was. She never saw me, and I never told her my name. I wasn't even sure of hers. I didn't know how to broach it in conversation – it would be embarrassing if she was offended that I didn't recognise her.

The guests must have thought I was suffering from some kind of paranoid anxiety, my eyes flicking back and forth between them, weighing each of them up in turn as if I suspected them of pouncing.

But as the ambrosial breakfast settled in my stomach, I let go. It was purer as a secret, as a mystery.

First published at www.eastoftheweb.com

I dreamt this, and woke up itching to write it down. Although the dream didn't get as far as the sex scene.

At the time of writing this story (2006), I was preoccupied with the idea that having too much freedom could actually hold you back, because you could become paralysed by choice.

Many people who read this story balk at the unprotected sex – but the unprotected sex is the story. The mysterious woman is intimidated by the infinite options that her freedom presents her, and is deliberately reckless with that freedom in the secret hope that the consequences will force a particular life path upon her, absolving her of responsibility for making the right choice.

The fact that I have to explain that means the story didn't really work, but I still like it.

HOW TO GET ANYTHING YOU WANT

I felt invincible. All the people I could persuade; all the long-held desires I could sate.

Today," she said, with that smile of hers trying to bust out of her face, "I am going to teach you how to get anything you want, from anyone, in three easy steps."

At that moment most of the men in the room only wanted one thing, and *she* had just volunteered to tell us how to get it. We were rapt.

"There are a few simple psychological tricks you can apply in any situation that'll guarantee you a high success rate," she continued with her lilting, frisky Cockney accent. She had the manner of an East End city girl, but something about her skin and bearing said she was born on a beach.

"The techniques are easy to use. By the end of this three-day course you'll be irresistibly persuasive. With a bit of practice you'll be selling timeshares to the dead."

It must work, I thought. After all, she had managed to persuade a roomful of people, myself included, to pay the best part of a grand to come on this course. I could not wait to find out how I had been duped into this.

"But first," she cooed, "let me introduce myself. My name is Joleen Moorcock. I worked for four years as chief training advisor with Kimberlever PLC before leaving to run these courses on my own. My interests include bikram yoga, which is yoga in high heat" – scantily clad in a sauna, contorting my body into the most fascinating positions (she only said this in my head) – "and raising money for charity. Next week I'm raising money for breast cancer research by walking a marathon in my bra, so I expect you all to support me."

This woman had the body of Barbie, the libido of Barbarella and the playfulness of Barbara Windsor. The ring on my wedding finger itched.

"Now let's go round the room and everyone else can introduce themselves. Let's start with you. What's your name and what do you do for a living?"

As she did the rounds I watched her lustfully, rampantly flexing my Deadly Sin. She had dark eyebrows and heavy eyelids, a small nose and a long, thin neck. Her curly black hair was pulled back into a cute-girl ponytail. And that smile – her face was built for it. It was a strain for her not to smile.

"Tom Burns," I said when it was my turn. "I'm a soap salesman."

"What are your hobbies?" she asked, her black eyes fixed on me.

Watching television and masturbating. It took me a few seconds to come up with something else. "Cooking. And reading," I said, which was almost true. Cooking Pot Noodles and reading *Loaded* magazine.

She flashed me a smile. She may have winked. I had to shuffle in my seat to hide my reaction. The rest of the room introduced themselves perfunctorily and I paid no attention to them whatsoever.

"Before I explain the first of the three steps," she said when the introductions were done, "I need you all to think of an example. An example of something that you want from someone – something that you've not been able to get, or that you think will be too difficult to get. Over the next three days you'll use this example to bring life to the techniques I'll teach you, and by the end of this course I guarantee you'll be able to get it, whatever it is."

She gave us a coffee break to think it over. I saw her drifting confidently from one conversation to another, making the course participants feel at ease. Laughing and smiling. Cheeky at both ends. She made me want her without even casting me a glance.

If I could get anything I wanted, from anyone, what would it be? Despite myself, I could only think of one example. I wanted Joleen. It seemed the perfect test of her technique; if she turned me down she would be admitting that her technique did not work. Then I could ask for my money back.

Of course, I never expected to succeed. No method of persuasion can be so magic as to fool the person who teaches it. Anyway, I would not want to succeed;

I was happily married. But there could be no harm in trying, could there?

I made my decision. I slipped off my wedding ring and hid it in my pocket.

"Has everyone thought of an example," she queried when the lesson restarted, "of something they really want?"

Bring it on, I thought.

She flicked on a PowerPoint slide. STEP 1. "The first step to persuading someone is getting them into a 'Yes' mind-set. We'll start with some basic principles, and then go into some specific psychological tricks."

At this stage I was extremely sceptical about the whole process. But as the day went on, I found myself impatient to try out the techniques on Joleen. Leading questions. Probing questions. Positive language. Body language. Using humour. Using silences. Matching the tone and pace of your target's voice. Letting your target talk about themselves (they will always think you interesting if you encourage them to talk about themselves). I was eager to put what I had learned to the test, so as soon as the course finished for the day, I cornered Joleen and got some real practice in.

Icebreaker question: "How long have you been running this course?" I asked her, casually.

"Oh," she said, smiling, "not very long really. Did you find today inspiring?"

Honesty: "I was cynical at first, but I'm coming round to it." *Open question:* "How did you learn the methods yourself?"

"A combination of things. I sort of compiled it from – well, you can't be interested really."

Getting her to talk about herself: "I am interested. Please go on . . ."

"Well, I did a lot of reading about persuasion techniques. A lot of my course is based on Chris de Lafley's series *Selling Sand to Saharans*, and I learned some of it from my work at Kimberlever."

Using humour: "I work for Doctor & Johnson, so I guess we're rivals." I made fists at her to illustrate this. I guess I thought it was funny. Mercifully, she laughed.

"Yes, you said you were a soap salesman, I remember. You're Tom."

"Tom Burns. Hi."

"Nice to meet you." She grinned.

Body language: I imitated her posture, then turned towards her and leaned forward. Reflexively, she turned towards me and leaned forward as well, bringing us comfortably closer together.

Getting a "Yes" mind-set: "Are you having supper in the hotel?"

"Yes," she said coquettishly.

"May I join you?"

"Yes."

Victory.

We talked for hours, about her mostly. We were interrupted only briefly when my wife called (I pretended she was my sister) to ask whether I thought it was a good idea to repaint the living room taupe.

Apart from that, the conversation flowed even better than the wine. I think Joleen was attracted to me; in my mind, at least. After supper and a glass or three at the bar, she made her excuses.

"I'd love to talk more," she purred, "but I have to prepare for tomorrow. I can't believe how late it is already. You've obviously mastered the rapport-building techniques from today's lesson – you had me here for ages longer than I meant to stay."

"That suits me, actually – I have to send a couple of work emails. We've got a very important new product release coming up," I boasted, "and I'm coordinating the launch."

"Really?" she said, leaning forward so her cleavage drew my eye. "What's the product?"

"It's a revolutionary new kind of soap, the cutting edge of technology really. You actually put it into your water supply, so the water that comes out of your shower or your bath taps already has this stuff dosed into it. It'll be a completely new category of product. I shouldn't be telling you all this, it's still top secret. The company even has a codename for it to fox our competition if they're spying on us."

Her glistening lips framed one of those winning grins. "These big companies get so paranoid about their new product developments, don't they?"

"Yes," I replied unnecessarily.

"And the codenames they give them are so funny sometimes, aren't they?"

"Yes." I laughed, knowingly.

"Like, what's the codename for this project?"

"Pigp–" I started, but I cut myself off. I sat back and slit my eyes. "Hey, I see what you're up to. You got me into a 'Yes' mind-set and asked me a question I shouldn't have answered."

Joleen was immediately apologetic, in her disarmingly effervescent way. "Sorry, I guess I do it instinctively now. I don't really care about your project. I suppose I'm just interested because I used to work in a similar area. I was just making conversation. Anyway, I'm off now. I'll see you tomorrow."

She said the last part with her hand resting affectionately on my shoulder. I was lost again in the allure of her smile. Still feeling the ghostly aftermath of pressure where her hand had been, I watched her glorious hips swaying as she walked away.

*

In the morning it was my head that was swaying. I struggled to pay attention to Joleen, who was as pert as ever.

"Getting whatever you want from people is about more than just getting them into a 'Yes' mind-set," she explained. "That'll get them on your side – they'll want to help you, they'll want to say yes to you – but if it's something they don't necessarily want to do, you still have to get around that. You have to make it sound like something they *do* want to do. You have to sell the idea to them. That's what today is about. Selling ideas."

Her words echoed in my head without sticking. I sat up and shook my head violently to clear it, resolving to make sense of what she was saying. She went on.

"Today I'm going to give you an extremely powerful tool called the Persuasion Model, which is basically a structured way of selling your ideas. The structure is compatible with the natural way that the human brain applies logic. It's actually designed to stimulate the neuronal responses involved in decision-making, making it very hard for the other party to disagree with you."

She explained that getting a "Yes" mind-set was just the first step, and the most important, of the Persuasion Model. She went through the other steps, including the magic phrases that tapped into your subconscious to make you want to say "Yes".

By the time the evening came I was burning to practise what I had learned. I found Joleen at the bar and bought her a drink. With a pint of bitter and the Persuasion Model as ammunition I felt quietly confident, and she seemed especially pleased to see me, which made me bolder still.

"Are you single?" I asked, recklessly.

"Yes." She grinned. "Why do you ask?"

A coy smile was enough of an answer.

"I'm quite picky about my men," she elaborated.

"What do you look for in a guy?"

As she talked, I revelled in her sex appeal. It took some concentration to prevent my brain from migrating about a metre down my body, but I managed to stay focused and apply every trick she had taught me to get her into a "Yes" mind-set. And I plied her with alcohol as a backup tactic. Soon I felt ready to go in for the kill.

I barrelled headlong into the Persuasion Model. The Model called for me to use the background knowledge I had gathered to come up with a compelling Hook, which would get Joleen irresistibly interested in my proposition: "If I could show you a way to have the night of your life, would you be interested?"

"Of course!" she cried.

"My idea is that you spend the night with me," I announced. I had worked her up into a "Yes" frenzy, but as soon as I announced my idea I saw her enthusiasm start to melt away. I rushed straight into the next step of the Persuasion Model.

"We'll spend one night together as a trial. There'll be no pressure. Tomorrow we'll act professionally, as if nothing happened. The key benefits are that you'll have satisfied your desire to be more spontaneous, you're guaranteed to have good conversation because you already know we have loads in common, and you'll have an intensely fun night."

The psychological ruses seemed to work unbelievably well. She was in a trance, as if everything but "Yes" had been systematically removed from her mind. I wrapped it up with the grand finale of the Persuasion Model, the Assumptive Close: "So, I'll meet you in Room 207 at ten?"

Her gorgeous jaw dropped open. She sat there, apparently stunned, seemingly trying to suppress an urge to nod her head vigorously. "That was masterful," she said at last. "I feel like I should say 'Yes' just to reward your effort. In fact, I can't think of a single reason not to sleep with you right now."

It was my turn for my jaw to drop. I never imagined this would actually work.

"I'll tell you what, Tom," she continued. "Just so I don't feel like I've given in too easily, I'll ask you a few questions to make sure we really have got loads in common. If I reckon you've answered them honestly, I'm yours for the rest of the night."

I could barely believe what she was saying. I would have thought she was kidding had she not been so damn sincere. I answered her first couple of questions automatically, before my brain had time to decide how to react.

"When's the last time you asked a woman out in a bar?" she asked.

"Never before," I said, my mind still racing.

"How important do you think it is to hold doors open for women?"

"It's only polite," I replied.

"Have you ever been unfaithful in a relationship?"

"No," I said, rather curtly. Not yet, I thought. I noticed her glancing at my wedding finger, which was bare.

Joleen leaned forward and undid the top button of her blouse. "One more question, and then you can do whatever you want with me." She licked her lips.

"What's the codename and release date of the Doctor & Johnson project you're working on?"

"That's got nothing to do with how much we have in common," I complained.

"You only have to answer if you want to have sex with me," she growled, and thrust her hand down my pants under the table. My resistance dissolved.

*

The next day I could not wipe the smile off my face. Guilty feelings did not get a look-in. She had been everything I could have hoped for. She had taken me to her hotel room and ravished me. She started by half-closing her eyes like a sultry siren, and stripping like a porn star. Then she kissed me and teased me, all the time asking me stupid questions about my job, like a game. Every time I answered her, she rewarded me until I was incoherent with lust. I relished her tawny skin, her forbidden charm.

And now she was lecturing the room as if nothing had happened, although I swear she gave me a conspiratorial glance once or twice. She was talking, in her gentle London twang, about what to do if you get a "No".

"However effective the Persuasion Model is," she explained, "it's not infallible. But, if you get a 'No', you can still turn it around. Today I'm going to show you how. First, you must establish the main genuine objection, which is often harder than it sounds . . ."

Her words washed over me. My mind was occupied with images and entanglements from the previous night.

I had no need to learn about handling objections – I was awed by the power of the Persuasion Model. I felt invincible. I was daydreaming about all the people I could persuade to do my bidding; all the long-held desires I could sate.

Of course above all I wanted to sleep with Joleen again. I wanted to repeat the illicit excitement of having someone new, someone secret, a match for my wildest fantasies. But she was playing coy with me all day, as she said she would. Even when we broke for lunch she managed to avoid me. I yearned for the day's end so I could speak to her alone.

As soon as Joleen announced the end of the course my heart leapt into my throat, and my brain leapt into my groin. She went round the room reviewing whether everyone was happy with the technique and had used it successfully. An impressive proportion said "Yes". She asked us to fill in feedback forms and tell all of our friends about the course, then she wished us goodbye and good luck.

While the mob filed out, I stayed behind on the pretence of checking the voicemail messages on my mobile phone. I did have one message, but it was only my wife. Joleen seemed oblivious of my presence as she packed away her papers and tidied up.

As soon as the last satisfied customer had left the room and the door had clicked shut behind him, Joleen looked up at me.

"Hi Tom." She grinned. Her cartoon smile had taken on a sinister nuance. I shifted uncomfortably in my seat, feeling suddenly vulnerable in this abandoned room dominated by such a predatory female. "I'm glad you stayed behind. You're my special student."

She put her papers down and sidled up to me, grabbing a chair so she could sit close, intimidating rather than intimate. I started quietly panicking – why was she being so unfriendly? Why the malice in her voice?

"I want to give you an extra lesson," she snarled with a bittersweet malevolence in her voice. "I have to admit that I didn't tell the whole truth on this course. Getting a 'Yes' mind-set, using the Persuasion Model, turning around a 'No' – those things are just shallow conjuring tricks. You can use them to persuade fools and children, but anyone with any sense will see through them.

"The good news is that there really *are* three easy steps to getting whatever you want, and they're much more powerful than the mumbo-jumbo I've taught you over the last three days. These three techniques are thousands of years old and have been proven against every type of person imaginable, from peasant to president."

Her body was still flirting, but her speech was portending doom. I had Trojan butterflies in my stomach.

"I'm going to teach you these steps, Tom: deception, bribery and blackmail. In fact, I've already shown you the first two. I deceived you by telling you that I no longer work for Kimberlever, and I bribed you with my body. In return, you told me some extremely valuable Doctor & Johnson company secrets. Now I want you to tell me the rest, so I'm going to demonstrate the third step. I'm going to blackmail you."

My head reeled at this news. My brain was struggling to assimilate the sight of sexy, playful Joleen, and the cold, calculating evil of what she was saying. I felt a creeping sense of my own stupidity at having let myself be manipulated by this woman, who had openly advertised herself as manipulative.

While I struggled to come to terms with the fact that I was suddenly a pawn in a twisted game of industrial espionage, she delivered her ultimatum. "I want you to bring me the formula card for this new product you're about to release, this Project Pigpen. You've probably never seen a formula card – it's an ordinary laminated A4 piece of paper, describing the exact chemical make-up and processes for manufacture of a product. It's usually kept in a vault at the factory where the product is made.

"You will meet me in the lobby of this hotel at 5pm exactly one week from now with a copy of the formula card, or I'll inform your manager that you've been divulging company secrets to the competition, and I'll describe our tryst last night to your wife. It might not be easy for you to get the formula card, but you can use the persuasion techniques I've taught you, especially the last three, to succeed. If you fail, you'll lose your job, your wife, everything. See you next week."

And with that, she gathered her things and left. I sat in my chair, mouth slightly open, until the janitor came in and started stacking chairs. Once again, I could not believe how comprehensively I had been screwed by this woman.

As I drove back home to my loving, unsuspecting wife, my mind worked through all the unwelcome possible outcomes of this situation. I imagined industrial tribunals, a messy divorce, financial hardship; I even entertained thoughts of murder and suicide. I was deep in the mire of my self-pity, indignant at the injustice of it all.

*

When I next saw Joleen I was full of conflicting emotion. I instantly remembered why I found her so attractive, and yet part of me was repulsed by her ever-present overconfident smirk. She was ordering a drink at the bar by the hotel lobby and she had not seen me yet. I tried to suppress my brain as it urged me to take violent revenge against her, and my other brain as it urged me to make vigorous love to her. I cleared my head, and put on a brave, happy face – both feelings so distant from the truth that I must have looked quite pained.

"Hi Joleen!" I chirped, brightly.

"Do you have it?" she asked coldly and cautiously.

"The formula card?" I queried innocently, sitting on a bar stool beside her and imitating her defensive posture.

"Yes," she replied.

I opened my arms and turned towards her slightly. Instinctively, she did the same. Let the games begin, I thought.

"I have it." I took it out of my briefcase and gave it to her in an envelope. She opened it and inspected it, at first suspicious, then quietly pleased. "I had a lot of fun getting it, actually," I continued. "You'd be very proud of me. I used all the tactics you taught. It is what you wanted, isn't it?"

"Yes," said Joleen, and she was about to say more but I kept talking.

"Great, I hope that puts me in the clear. Although I've been thinking – you have it made, don't you? You must get *two* salaries. One from running the course, and one from Kimberlever." I left a silence. She made no reply and the silence stretched. It felt uncomfortable, but she herself had taught me that silences were a great way of getting people to talk and say things that they may not otherwise have said.

"That's none of your business," she snapped at last, and I started speaking again before she could go on.

"Well, I guess that makes you a very rich and successful woman," I flattered. "I admire that. And you're beautiful as well. I feel like the luckiest man alive to have slept with you, even if it was only to get me to tell you all that stuff about Doctor & Johnson." I hoped I had not gone too far. I put my hand on her knee and played up my doe-eyed devotion for her, and I seemed to get away with it.

"Don't think that I'll sleep with you again," she warned, pushing my hand away.

I braced myself and dived into the deep end: "If I could show you a way to make even more money without having to seduce nobodies like me, would you be interested?"

I had said it with just enough eagerness and sincerity to catch her off guard.

"Go on . . ." she coaxed warily.

"My idea is that I continue to provide you with Doctor & Johnson company secrets, in return for a cut of the pay you get from Kimberlever." Now I had her attention. I went on to the next step of the Persuasion Model.

"With my inside knowledge I can provide you with twice as much information as you're getting now, so you can ask for twice as much money. In return all I ask is forty percent. On balance you'll be richer, and you never have to pay attention to a sap like me again."

She was quiet. I had persuaded her to consider the proposition, already further than I had expected to get, although I was still heart-stoppingly nervous inside. I gave her a few seconds to think it over, then went for an Assumptive Close.

"Here's my business card. Email me a maildrop address and I'll start posting you the information right away."

Her face was almost blank. I could not tell if that was because everything but "Yes" had been removed from her mind, or if it was because she was about to laugh in my face.

"Not so fast," she whispered. "How do I know Kimberlever will give me a pay rise for this? I'll give you twenty percent."

My heart leapt. I was swept with a relief so strong it was almost sickening. I rejoiced inside and relaxed without. Joleen could immediately tell that there was something wrong.

"Tom?" she managed, reproachfully.

"Joleen," I countered, "you're an absolute genius."

She looked horrified.

"Your techniques to get anything you want are amazing. They even worked on you." I pulled my mobile phone out of my pocket. I had recorded her confession. "You'll be pleased to know that I applied your excellent teachings to deceive and bribe you, and now I'm going to blackmail you. You see, that formula card isn't for Project Pigpen, it's for ordinary household soap. I got it from my A-level physics textbook. That was my deceit. Then I bribed you with the possibility of making more money. I guess as someone so motivated by ruthless greed, you just assumed I was motivated by the same thing, otherwise I'm sure I wouldn't have been able to convince you."

"And you recorded our whole conversation, which you're going to use to blackmail me," she spat bitterly.

"That's right!" I was quite excited by then. "If this gets to the Office of Fair Trading, they'll make sure you never work again, and if this leaks to the media, you'll be publicly discredited as a business spy whore. That'd make a good headline, don't you think?"

"What do you want?" she demanded.

I took a deep, satisfied breath. I reminded myself not to be too greedy, not to let the power of the victory go to my head. "All I want is to remove you from my life, forever, as if you'd never existed. If I ever see you again, if my wife ever thinks I had an affair, if Kimberlever sabotages Doctor & Johnson's launch – if any of those things happen, I'll send this recording out."

I could see a train of four-letter words that exploded behind her smouldering black eyes, but the one that she voiced was, "Done." With that, she got up and left to take her temper out on something else.

I sighed peacefully and ordered a celebratory drink. Perhaps the power of getting anything you want is too dangerous for human hands; after all, I got what I wanted and it nearly ruined me. For the time being, I thought, I would stick to simply asking for what I wanted. That way I would be protected from getting it.

This story got me fired.

In 2004 I was working for Procter & Gamble as a field-based sales account manager. I didn't have my own computer, so I wrote this story on my company laptop. When the laptop went in for an update, I was called in for an urgent meeting at head office, so I drove down right away from Birmingham to Surrey.

I was marched into a meeting room and informed that I had committed gross misconduct. My employment was terminated, effective immediately. They took my building pass, my company mobile, and the keys to my company car, and called security to escort me off the premises. I had to walk to the train station to get back home.

The thing they were so upset about was that I'd been using my company laptop to store personal files. They took particular offence at a picture of me pretending to smoke a spliff, some very vanilla pornography, and – above all – this story.

THE CUT

Feda wanted to say a hundred things, but one rose above the others. "I've been cut."

Feda admired his father. Gurion was a woodworker and joiner of a skill unmatched this side of Ngoro. He could make a plank straight and level enough to satisfy the gods themselves – the elder women demanded it to show their dominion over nature – but he was happiest, as now, making peasant furniture that respected the grain of the wood.

The backrest of the chair he was working on now was a single slice from the base of a red sapele tree, its concentric age lines drawing the eye hypnotically into its centre. Gurion had sheltered and smoked the piece for over a month to dry without cracking. In the humidity of the jungle, it was said, the driest things were Gurion's wood and Mother mRoto's humour.

Gurion knelt, bracing the slice of wood between his legs, cutting precise notches into one edge with a chisel and hammer, being careful to apply force in just the right direction. Feda had learned his father's trade and hoped one day to be as skilled a craftsman as he, but for now his job was to gather the shavings for kindling.

This was to be Feda's ritual chair. It would be complete by sundown, but it would not really be finished until it had been splashed with Feda's blood. Gurion shifted his weight into a squat. Feda knew that his father found it uncomfortable to kneel for too long since having undergone the ritual of manhood himself, many monsoons ago.

Once, he had asked his father exactly what the ritual involved. Gurion had slipped with his plane and ruined a fine headboard. In all the cursing and scolding, Feda's question had been lost, but he knew better than to ask again. Feda knew only that the ritual involved a cut, a cut in his most private and sensitive part, and it was bound up in his head with desire, pain, fear, belonging, becoming.

Having completed the joint, Gurion mixed a paste of sap and crushed leaves until it had the texture of semen. Feda filled his head with the carnal smell. He became self-conscious of his crotch.

Feda asked his father, "Does it hurt for long?"

A gobbet of the paste Gurion was using to glue the joint fell to the ground. "The pain is the price of manhood. You'll be given to a wife. You'll make a home. You'll have a profession."

Feda wondered what it felt like to be a man. He knew there were secrets between grown men and women, and he was curious to see how this cut would help him discover them.

At that moment Mother mPene appeared. "Gurion!" she reprimanded. "Why are you still working on the ritual chair? Tromo is coming tomorrow."

"I know, I know. I'll make eight more chairs."

"Make them now!"

"Tromo's chairs will not be sat in tomorrow. Feda's will. The glue needs as long as possible to set."

Tromo with his big-city clothes, his computers, his smell like a carrion flower.

"Make ten more chairs!"

"I've only planed the wood for eight."

"Make twelve more chairs!"

Gurion looked at his feet. "Yes, Mother."

mPene gave a curt nod. "Feda, walk with me."

"But I need his help," Gurion protested.

"Gurion, come to bed tonight when you're done. Don't wake me. Feda, walk."

Feda obeyed, head down. mPene held Feda's hand and led him through the vines, past the children playing with hoops and sticks, around the big cooking pit and into her hut.

She sat Feda down and fixed him with a disquietingly benign gaze. She was silent for a long while. Feda kept his back straight and tried not to fidget.

"Tomorrow you'll become a man. Prior Lami will administer the cut."

"But why?" Feda asked, and immediately regretted it. He knew that women had their own blood rite bestowed upon them by nature, and to challenge the necessary act of balancing was churlish. But mPene was not angry.

"Your penis is a disgusting thing, young Feda, and as you age it becomes far worse. The most evil sins in your soul become concentrated upon it and manifest as scurf beneath your foreskin. Lust, anger, greed, envy, pride. By cutting these free your soul is released to allow you to take your proper place in the community, as a man serving his Mothers and his wife."

"Who will be my wife?"

"Mother mRoto's eldest granddaughter, mFana, has chosen you."

Feda's ears burned red. Mother mFana! Surely the most desirable young woman in the village. Certainly beautiful. He felt his crotch stir with excitement and was immediately ashamed.

"I feel . . . fearful."

mPene became stern. "Don't let me down, Feda, my child."

She stood and Feda took his cue to leave.

That night as Feda lay on his bed, he pressed his nails into his foreskin, trying to persuade himself that the pain would pass quickly. Then he thought of mFana's silken skin and felt himself becoming aroused. He turned to lie on his stomach, pressing his growing shame against the rattan, willing it to recede again.

The ritual the next day was performed with little ceremony. Gurion, his eyes swollen, presented Feda with his chair; the chair was carried into Prior Lami's medical tent and Feda followed feeling numb to his fate.

Lami was a skinny man with hollow eyes, skin like biltong, and a permanently amused expression. He had been administering the ritual cuts for this village and the next for two decades. He smelled faintly of iron.

"You must be completely naked," he said, facing away from Feda and laying out his tools. He turned a moment later. "Come on, come on."

Feda took his clothes off and sat. He took comfort in the chair, knowing that his father had expended much effort and love making it for him. He looked down at his genitals. A sorry-looking slug hiding in straggly moss. At that moment he hated them and they did not feel part of him.

Lami pushed Feda's knees apart and knelt between his legs. Deftly, he tied a string tightly around the middle of Feda's penis. Feda gasped at the sudden constriction. Sweat pricked at his brow. Lami produced a tool that looked like Tromo's cigar cutter, a miniature guillotine.

Feda's penis was threaded through the device, which pushed his foreskin back so that the tip of his penis was fully visible, looking like a closed cup mushroom. There was a smart clicking sound like a hammer tapping the end of a chisel, and Feda had the sudden sensation that he had wet himself. Dismayed, he moved his hands to cover himself, but Lami batted him away.

"You're bleeding," said Lami flatly, preparing a hasty poultice. "Be still."

Feda focused and saw that where the end of his penis had once been, there was now a river of blood. He jumped out of his seat, tugging at the severed stump between his legs.

"You cut off too much! You cut off too much!"

"Idiot child!" scolded Lami. "Sit on your hands and let me stem the bleeding. You're aggravating it. Sit down!"

Feda sat, not out of obedience but because his balance felt suddenly compromised and his vision became dim – or rather, white, as if the sun shone directly in his eyes. His legs squirmed beneath him as he struggled to bear the agony in his groin, which sucked up his whole being like a black hole.

Feda was vaguely aware of Lami talking as he pulled and pinched at the terrible wound. He forced himself to hear the words.

"Crazy child," Lami muttered, shaking his head and half grinning. "You think I'd cut too much? I've been doing this since before you were born. I cut every man in this tribe. I cut your father, just the same amount. Now, hold still."

Lami might have said more, but just then a stab of pain more severe than Feda could have imagined possible consumed his very soul. He threw his head back and uttered a soundless howl. He felt his consciousness falter, but it stubbornly remained.

"OK, all done," said Lami. "Now get up."

Feda jerked his head forward and, sweating and grinding his teeth, he glared wide-eyed at Lami's face. Had he heard correctly?

"Come on, up, up. Go to your father. I will bring the chair so you can rest a while." Lami hoisted Feda to his feet, helped him into a robe and escorted him out of the tent.

As he crossed to his father's hut, Lami at his side dragging his ritual chair, Feda cast his eyes about like a wounded dog. Could it be that all these men, casually going about their business, had each been so violently trimmed? It seemed impossible that he would ever be able to function normally again.

Upon reaching Gurion's hut he staggered to his room and sat on the proffered chair, swallowing the bile that rose in his throat when he saw the jagged trails of blood that now decorated the wood.

Lami took his leave and Gurion appeared. For a few seconds father and son locked eyes, but such was the vehemence of the unspoken words that passed between them, Gurion had to look away.

"Father!" accused Feda.

Gurion looked pained, but could not speak. He rallied, but again the words did not come. In the end, he nodded, eyes still downcast, and he left.

Feda gingerly transferred himself to his rattan bed, and then a moment later back to the chair, and then he stood and leaned his head against the wall, and then he crouched, and lay on the floor, and repeated the whole cycle again. Relief utterly eluded him. Each passing minute stretched for an hour, an hour felt like a week.

At some point Gurion brought him food, for which he had no appetite. Despite a scorching thirst he refused to drink any water. He must have slept for he woke startled by nightmares of peeing a painful spray of urine and blood.

Eventually – it might have been the next morning, although Feda had lost track of time – he was able to persuade himself that the pain was becoming a thing outside of him, a thing he could begin to put aside. He began to be able to think of other things. He toyed with the idea of leaving his room and getting something to eat.

But then he received a visitor.

mFana sashayed into his room while he was trying to dress. He put Lami's robe back on and turned to greet her. Her face was round and inviting, with a smile that could coax a blossom from a stone. Feda started saying something but his tongue became fat in his mouth.

"Feda, you're to be my husband," she said. He felt a childish love for the dimples in her cheeks. Her beaded hair and scent of shea nuts. Her body like a wood-carved sculpture. "If you're loyal, I'll repay you with a thousand kindnesses. I'll protect and defend you. I'll satisfy you and make you proud. Help me to make a home and it will be our spring of contentment."

Feda wanted to say a hundred things, but one rose above the others.

"I've been cut."

"Yes, I know. It'll take some time to heal. And then we can start our family." She rested a hand on her midriff. A flash of endearing mischief crossed her face, and she quietly closed the door to the room.

She gently pushed Feda down into his chair and stood above him. With one fluid movement she removed her camisole. Her skin was smooth as a wax leaf. Her breasts a perfect handful. Her nipples like kola nuts.

But Feda's lustful trance was quickly overtaken by sudden alarm. He felt his penis becoming erect, and panicked, leaping to his feet. mFana laughed at him. He could feel the wound reopening and felt sick with the anticipated pain. With urgency she put her finger to her lips, dressed herself and left.

Again, the sensation of having wet himself. A crimson stain spread quickly across his robe. He whipped the robe off and stared at the blood pumping copiously out of the hole. He screamed. Loud enough to boil the river, he screamed.

He was only dimly aware of what happened next. His mind swam with disturbing visions; his body writhed constantly as if he were a snake shedding its skin. He allowed himself to be moved and manipulated without thinking to question why or who. Despite the oppressive heat, he shivered with cold. Trembled with thirst. Swam in sweat.

In brief moments of clarity he knew that he had succumbed to fever, brought on by an infection. The infection manifested in his mind as a parasitic scorpion in his lap. Several times he brushed the beast away, but the pain of its sting persisted.

At last, after some days, he woke feeling terrible, but once again present. A soothing compress rested against his forehead. Gurion sat by his bedside, holding his hand.

"Welcome back," whispered Gurion.

With his father's help, Feda was able to get out of bed to eat, wash and relieve himself. He could no longer pee standing up, he had to squat, and even then it was impossible not to get urine on his legs. He cleaned himself carefully, neglecting only the truncated stub of his penis which was still too tender to touch.

He found himself walking with shorter strides, even long after the pain had subsided. His whole stature had been somehow altered. He started helping his father with his woodworking again, lamely at first like a decrepit elder, but then increasingly with his former youthful vigour.

One day Mother mPene declared him fully recovered, and announced that he and mFana would be married that weekend. mFana had not seen him much, having been busy harvesting coffee and qat, but with the wedding date set she became attentive, visiting him every evening and quietly watching him plane wood with Gurion. They were shy with each other.

On the morning of the wedding, there was electricity in the air. All the women of the village wore wraparound trousers of white linen, and ruched tops that accentuated the white teeth of their smiles. The men wore three-quarter shorts and diaphanous shirts in bold colours. Everyone had a dance in their step.

mFana held herself with grace and pride, frills at her sleeves and dyed feathers in her hair. Feda felt real awe at the sight of her; fear and wonder in equal measure. She was beautiful.

As was the tradition, the marital tent was designated. The people of the village stood by it in a circle, with Feda and mFana on opposite sides. Gurion and Mother mRoto led their respective offspring into the middle, nodded solemnly to each other, and entered the tent to negotiate the terms of the marriage.

The circle was quiet and still. In the centre, Feda and mFana locked eyes, but they were not permitted to touch. At first it felt uncomfortable to look so directly into a woman's eyes, but with infinitesimal gestures she coaxed him to relax.

mFana's eyes were deep and soft, full of intimacy, reassurance, perhaps even love. Feda asked those eyes a thousand questions, and the answer was singular: Trust, Feda. Trust.

Feda was stirred from his reverie by a sudden restlessness in the assembled crowd. mRoto and Gurion emerged from the tent, laughing gaily. Old Mother mRoto, her kindly face lined like windblown sand, raised a banana leaf above her head and muttered a prayer in the ancient tongue.

With the leaf she bound the couple's hands, and thus they were joined.

Immediately, the circle broke into cheers and dance. A fire was lit, food appeared, music played – djembe drums. The party would be wild and long. But Feda would not join in the revelry, for he had an important obligation to fulfil. A gentle pull on his arm from mFana told him that she was very keen to fulfil it.

She led him into the marital tent, which was empty save for a washbowl and a makeshift bed. Feda's stomach constricted. He only vaguely understood what was going to happen next, and the thought of it made him want to flee.

"Come," said mFana, sitting on the bed. "Kiss me, my husband."

Feda obliged. Their lips touched and opened. Her tongue flicked out like a snake's. Feda found himself distracted by the raucous sound of celebration just outside the tent. mFana laughed and the kiss was broken.

"Feda, husband, you are stiff as one of Gurion's planks. Come to me. Forget yourself." As she said this, she put her hand between Feda's legs. Feda knew he should submit, but he could not help squirming away.

"I don't want you to see," he said.

"Nonsense." She pulled his shorts down. She examined him, smiled tightly, and held his severed member tenderly. Feda stood stock still as if facing down a lioness. His throat was dry.

mFana removed her top and untied her wraparound trousers, letting them fall to the ground. She began touching herself, caressing her breasts. In her growing excitement she grabbed at Feda's penis.

"Ow!"

"Sorry. I'll be gentle." But she persisted, tugging at Feda until he became firm. Feda looked at his erect half-penis with bile in his throat. It was purple, lumpy-scarred and disgusting. But mFana didn't seem to notice as she guided Feda to lie on top of her and enter her.

Her eyes closed. She pressed his hips into her, and massaged her clitoris furiously. Feda's teeth gritted. He matched her rhythm, to help her reach satisfaction as quickly as possible. He tried closing his eyes, but saw a ghostly vision of his wound reopening and then had to check several times to convince himself that the moisture he felt was neither blood nor urine but mFana's natural lubrication.

She moaned; her face creased into something like an expression of pain. Feda realised his face was similarly creased and he made a conscious effort to relax, without success. But there was something, despite the discomfort, something primal and attractive about this difficult, sweaty act. It reminded him of the one and only time he had tried smoking a cigarette – it had been revolting, yet as soon as he had finished he had been tempted to have another.

At last she climaxed and released him. He immediately sat up and inspected himself for damage. He turned away, ashamed to let mFana see his distress.

"You didn't finish," breathed mFana.

"Sorry. I'm a little sore."

"Ah, well, it's your first time." mFana sat up and hugged him. Her voice was affectionately mocking. "But you're going to have to do better next time, husband, if I'm to become pregnant."

Feda tried to take comfort in her embrace. He listened to the sounds of the party outside, and watched the flickering shadows cast against the sides of the tent by dancers in the firelight.

Married life started well. mFana was loving and considerate, and seemed pleased with Feda. He moved into her family residence, a large clay-brick house with individual bedrooms for Mother mRoto and three of her grandchildren: mFana and her younger sisters mGele and little Kampa. Feda was not used to the household's noise and bustle and welcomed the relative peace of his daily work with Gurion.

mFana became increasingly aggressive during their lovemaking until they found a reliable way of making Feda productive. When at last mFana fell pregnant, Feda wrestled with his conscience until he could no longer allow propriety to hold him back; while they rested in bed, he blurted out his ultimatum.

"If we have a son, we must not cut him."

Only after he had said it did he realise how heretical and dangerous the idea was, and yet how firmly he believed it. In the face of Mother mFana's silence he simultaneously wanted to defend his position, and undo it. The silence stretched for so long he wondered if she was pretending he had not spoken at all. But the mien of her body told otherwise.

Then she turned away from him. "I've decided," she said. "You will become a qat farmer."

"What? But I'm a woodworker and joiner like my father. That's my talent, that's what I love. I've started making my own chairs already, and Tromo says they're very fine. There's good money in that."

"You will become a qat farmer," she repeated, in a tone that invited no response.

Feda was baffled, until slowly he understood that he had been punished for rebelling against the ritual cut, even if only by thought. He was crestfallen. Sleep was elusive for him that night as his mind revisited the injustice endlessly in a self-amplifying spiral.

Thus Feda began learning a new trade. There was much to learn, and it so absorbed him at first that he was sometimes able to forget how much he missed working with wood. During this time, Feda grew closer to mFana's younger sisters, serving as a father figure although they were almost adults themselves. In the cool season little Kampa started menstruating and became Mother mKampa.

mKampa in particular seemed to admire Feda, and frequently flattered him with challenging questions about how the world worked, which he took great pride in answering in the most direct and practical way possible. She asked where the rain came from, and where it went. She asked why people valued money so much when it had no inherent usefulness. She asked what it was like to live in different parts of the world. Feda answered everything, glossing over details he wasn't sure of.

Once, when they had both wakened early and were sitting together on the terrace, she dropped her voice to ask him about the ritual cut.

"It's our way of balancing nature," he replied. "And tempering the male weakness for ego and violence."

"How can it do all that?" she said. "Anyway, you don't seem convinced."

"It's been this way for generations."

"But what's actually cut? Ego and violence come from the heart, how can they be tempered by cutting a little finger – whether it's on your hand or between your legs?"

"A penis is more than a finger. It gathers . . ." Feda hesitated, trying to recall what Mother mPene had said about his foreskin. "Now, see. The evil thoughts of men physically gather as pus around the end of the penis. So the end of the penis is cut off."

He had tried to sound authoritative, but mKampa clearly saw through his act. "That's brutal!" she spat. "Didn't you think to protest?"

Feda blinked hard to suppress his emotion. "It's a high price to pay."

"To pay for what? My children will never suffer such degradation. I'll temper their violence and ego by teaching them, not maiming them."

Feda remained silent.

"I refuse to believe it," she said. "Show me."

Feda shook his head and stayed put, but did not dare to object. Even in her youth, this girl already had the practised and petulant authority of a Mother.

"Show me," she repeated.

"I must go now," said Feda.

He stood, but did not immediately leave. He desperately wanted to communicate how he felt: his gratitude that she too suspected the cut was an unconscionable hypocrisy; his fear that her innocent fervour would be tainted and forgotten as she grew. But how to put it into words? How to trust her?

mKampa's bright eyes shone up at him. She nodded, and Feda's heart bloomed with hope that she had understood. But in fact she had gravely misunderstood. Before Feda had a chance to react, she lifted her hands and pulled down his shorts.

"No!" he cried, but it was too late. She screwed up her face and grunted in disgust. Feda covered himself and sat, his cheeks flushing.

mKampa opened her mouth to speak, but at that moment Mother mRoto appeared on the terrace and shouted, "What are you doing?"

"Oma, he showed me his cut. I –"

"He showed you? He *showed* you?"

"She did it," Feda retorted, but this angered Mother mRoto even more. She roared, and slapped him.

"Get out of this house! Go!"

Feda ran. He beat his fist against his forehead as he headed into the jungle, squashing the dewy detritus underfoot. Reeling, he instinctively headed to Gurion's hut.

Gurion was there, as always, with his piles of wood ready to be cut and planed. He saw the tears on his son's face and instinctively knew that whatever trouble this was, it was deep. Wordlessly, he handed Feda an adze and gestured for him to sit and work the wood with him.

For the next hour, neither of them spoke as they worked side by side. Then the police came.

"Police?" said Gurion.

Feda shook his head. But they were police, two imposing women, stern and sweating in their uniform.

"Feda Agbola," said the broader of the two, "you're under arrest for adultery and fornication."

"I didn't commit adultery. I didn't even touch her."

"You must come with us."

"No. I refuse to accept the charge."

"Then get yourself a lawyer. We have a telephone at the station."

Feda looked pleadingly at his father. Gurion's mouth was slightly open, his busy hands still. When Feda's shoulders dropped, the police pulled him to his feet, and cuffed his wrists behind his back.

As they took Feda away, Gurion said only, "I love you."

For the next two days, Feda was kept in a solitary cell with almost no communication with the outside world. The cage served as an echo chamber for his shame and righteous rage. By the time of his trial he brimmed with hatred, aimed both outwardly and in.

Thirsty and dirty, he railed at the police officer who escorted him to the court. There, he met his lawyer, a sharply dressed city Mother on a community-volunteering ticket. She asked for his story, which he told in detail although she looked summarily unconvinced. In the end, she advised him to say as little as possible.

The trial felt like a fantasy. Feda could not assimilate that the person being spoken of was himself. On one side of the courtroom sat most of the Mothers of the village, including mFana and mKampa; on the other side sat Gurion, Prior Lami and two strangers.

The prosecutor began by describing the events of the morning in question, concluding with: "Having seduced Mother mKampa, you prepared to copulate, with your wife's youngest sister no less. The act was interrupted by your wife's grandmother, but your intention was clear. You have viciously betrayed the trust placed in you by your devoted wife. What's more, you are cowardly enough to blame Mother mKampa. For such a flagrant breach of common morality you should suffer the most terminal penalty allowed by law."

The case for the defence rested on downgrading the charge from adultery and fornication to indecent exposure, which did not sit easily with Feda. Even the best possible outcome would be a gross injustice.

The cross-examination was particularly painful.

"Immediately prior to you exposing your genitals, were you having a heated debate about the legitimacy of the cut?" asked the prosecutor.

"She was –"

"Yes or no answers, please."

". . . Yes."

"Were you feeling angered and resentful about having undergone the cut?"

"No."

"So you approve of the cut?"

Feda did not answer.

"Is it true that you have in the past insisted to your wife that any sons of yours would not have the cut?"

Feda looked at the floor. "Yes."

"I put it to you that you were angry and resentful about the cut. You blamed your wife and wished to betray her out of vengeance and contempt."

"No!"

These manipulations continued, on and on, casting Feda as a lying, impulsive, conniving deviant. The spectating Mothers occasionally gasped and tutted, mFana loudest of all. Only mKampa was still, her expression inscrutable as she sat silently absorbing the proceedings. Whether she was protecting herself, or perhaps believed the prosecutor's argument that she had been exploited, Feda did not know.

The defence seemed weak in comparison, like trying to apply a sticking plaster to a shattered soul. But, after what seemed like hours, the judge accepted the defence. Feda was found innocent of adultery and fornication, but guilty of indecent exposure and breach of marital contract. The sentence was five years' imprisonment and mandated divorce. Feda would have plenty of time to reflect on his hollow victory.

The nearest prison was in the city, over a hundred miles away. His time there passed slowly. He resolved that as soon as he could think clearly he would reflect on how he had ended up here and what he could learn. But these revelations never came; each day was a paler imitation of the last, until his will atrophied. Five years seemed like a lifetime.

Worse than prison was returning home. He had changed. His small community seemed alien and hostile to him now. Even the things that used to comfort him felt empty. No one was uncivil to him, and he was allowed to work wood with Gurion again, yet he keenly felt his status as an outcast.

Not long after Feda's return, his son had his fifth birthday. Feda was not invited to see him. So when Tromo came to buy Gurion and Feda's furniture, Feda asked for a ride to the city.

In the truck he asked Tromo if he had been cut.

"Of course," said Tromo. "Every man is cut."

Feda sighed disconsolately. "Then the city is not far enough for me. Take me to the port."

Eight years later, Prior Lami administered to Feda's son the ritual cut.

First published in The Mechanics' Institute Review Issue 14 (Birkbeck, 2017)

Written in 2016.

I was disgusted to discover how many girls and women suffer from female genital mutilation (FGM), even in my own country. I wanted to write a story that reflected the horror and insidiousness of this crime. I flipped the genders because I wanted men in particular to squirm.

After this story was published, I read part of it aloud at an event in Camden. I enjoyed watching the faces of a group of strangers as I described cutting a penis in half.

GO

❝
I believed him. I believed that by becoming better at this game, I would become a better person.
❞

A few years ago, a man called Sensei introduced me to the game of go.

I had just moved into the area and I was scoping out the local pub on a quiet Sunday afternoon. The pub was very traditional, with dark-wood furniture in a cosy cluster around a real fire. He was sitting alone in a corner with two small wicker baskets in front of him, each the size of a honeydew melon.

We made brief eye contact and he smiled. He had friendly black eyes and a short greying beard. He wore a plain black shirt, open at the collar as if he was winding down after a hard day's work. His aura was calm, lonely. I felt drawn to him.

I approached the bar near him and ordered a beer. While it was being poured, I turned and asked him what was in the baskets.

He lifted the lid off one, revealing hundreds of small white stones inside. They reflected the dancing light from the fire. I stared at them, captivated. I glanced up at the man, and he nodded. I plunged my hand into the basket and felt the smooth, glass stones parting and surrounding my fingers. Wonderful.

"What are they for?" I asked.

"A game."

I paid for my drink and pointed at his table. "May I?"

He nodded. "I'd welcome company. I've been expecting a friend, but he hasn't come."

I sat, and put my hand back into the basket of stones. I pulled one out. It was lenticular, slightly larger than a pound coin, and it had a subtle but pleasing weight to it.

"These are game pieces?"

He opened the other basket, which contained hundreds of little black stones. "Yes. An ancient game from the Far East."

As I picked out one of the black stones, I noticed that there was a board on the table. It was wood, a slightly lighter shade than the table, with thin painted lines dividing it up into hundreds of squares. Experimentally, I placed the black stone I was holding onto the board. It landed with a satisfying clack.

"No, my friend." The man smiled, shifting my piece. "You play on the intersections, not inside the squares." He picked up a white stone and placed it on the opposite side of the board to my black stone.

"What's the aim of the game?" I asked.

"To surround more empty territory than your opponent."

188

"Can I move the stones?"

"No, we just keep adding stones until all the territory is claimed."

We each played three more stones. I put mine next to each other so they started to surround a corner. "But what if you play inside my territory?" I asked.

"If you surround one of my stones, or a group of my stones, without leaving any spaces, those stones are removed from the board. I'll show you."

He played a few moves ahead, placing stones for both of us, to demonstrate.

"That's it," he said. "You now know everything you need to play the game of go."

"Go," I repeated. I swirled the word around in my mind. There was something about this time, this place, this man . . . I felt an affinity for this game without yet understanding it. I played another piece.

We played for hours, although it passed all too quickly. At closing time, as we left the pub, I asked the man his name. He said I was to call him Sensei. I thanked him and headed home.

On Monday morning I settled back into my routine, filling my brain with spreadsheets and reports. But at the back of my mind was an image that I could not shake off, of Sensei and me playing go in that quiet, old-fashioned pub. Every now and then I thought I could smell that aroma of ale and wood. I craved another game.

When Sunday came around, I went back to the pub, aching to learn more about this game. To my delight, Sensei was there, alone, smiling as if he had expected me.

"My friend hasn't turned up again," he said.

"Teach me," I appealed. He pushed the basket of black stones towards me, and we played.

It was such a simple game, but the ease with which he dominated me told me it had far more depth than I could possibly appreciate yet. And it was beautiful. An expansive board, punctuated by minimalist swathes of black and white, like a binary work of art.

I was focusing so completely on the board that the world seemed to end beyond its boundaries. I felt like I was pursuing something so purely intellectual that the demands of the physical world faded away.

"You're forgetting, friend," said Sensei, lifting me from my reverie. "The aim of the game is to surround empty space. Capturing stones is just a tool. If you make capturing stones your aim, you'll lose."

As we played on, he occasionally imparted advice and ruminations. I imagined him as a hundred-year-old Japanese go master, with a long white beard, teaching wisdom in haikus. I imagined flute music in the background, like in old samurai films. Of course, he wasn't Japanese and there was no music, but the game seemed to conjure up an atmosphere of its own.

"Go is the oldest board game that still exists today," he said as we played. "It's been played in the Orient since the Bronze Age, and it's as popular there as it ever was. But it hasn't taken off in the West. Western culture favours games like chess, where the object is to destroy your opponent, rather than go, where the object is to negotiate shared territory."

Again, we played until closing time. I felt like I hadn't even scratched the surface – I had a lot to learn.

That night, and almost every night that week, I dreamt of go. Of the shapes the pieces made; of the invisible influence each group had; of the maths and the art of the game.

The following Sunday Sensei started teaching me how to recognise common shapes, and how to identify whether they were good or bad. I started to learn a whole new vocabulary: ladders and liberties, eyes and walls, thickness and empty triangles, life and death. I learned words in a new language: ko, atari, aji, moyo, gote, sente. The more I learned the more I had a sense that I knew nothing.

The infinite complexity and subtleties of the game astounded me, particularly because they arose from such straightforward rules. This was surely the purest game ever invented.

"Don't get distracted by the small buzzes of activity," Sensei scolded as we played. "Sometimes it's wiser to rise above a small threat and play elsewhere, where you can gain much more in the long term. Go is a game of balance on several levels. In many ways, it reflects life itself."

I believed him. I believed that by becoming better at this game, I would become a better person. I would learn to rise above things that were not a real priority; I would learn new ways to approach the conflicting demands of life.

We played for many Sundays, and not once did I beat him. But our scores at the end of each game drew closer and closer.

After we finished each game, the final arrangement of stones was like a map of our minds; a record of successes and defences, invasions and false starts. A bittersweet snapshot of gains and losses, hopes and dreams.

Sometimes it occurred to me that I knew almost nothing about Sensei. He always looked a little dishevelled. He did not wear a wedding ring. He spent every Sunday afternoon in a pub with no company except me. I might infer from that sparse knowledge that he was a lonely and insecure man. But I never asked. To me he was an omniscient mentor with a rich history and boundless patience. It would have broken my heart to believe anything else.

Months passed, and I never missed a Sunday with Sensei. He seemed to have an endless reserve of wisdom and anecdotes, and an infinite capacity to outwit me on the go board.

Then, one Sunday afternoon when we were both just a little bit older, as winter was setting in and the warmth of the fire enveloped us, I played my perfect game.

It was the third game of the evening, and it would have to be the last because the pub was closing soon. I felt inspired; I felt like I could see the invisible influences of every single piece; I felt like I could divine all of Sensei's secret intentions and pre-empt them.

I could see that he was impressed. He was taking longer to think for each of his moves. For that fleeting moment, I felt like we were having the most significant battle in the world.

We fought to the very end. I felt physically exhausted as I placed the final, climactic stones on the board. The remaining dashes of empty territory were small, and I could not tell who had more.

I held my breath as we accounted for the captured stones and counted out our score. Twenty-two points each. A draw.

"Very rare, to have a draw," said Sensei with raised eyebrows. He smiled broadly and looked up at me. "Next time, you play white and I'll go first."

My heart was beating hard as adrenalin coursed through me. My chest was bursting with pride. For the first time, I felt like I understood this game. I felt like I had a chance of mastering it. I wanted to hug Sensei. Instead, I put my hand on his arm, just to touch him.

As we put the pieces away, he talked. "Many people consider the aesthetics of the game to be almost as important as the gameplay. Indeed, much thought has been given to the design. The spaces on the board are slightly rectangular, so that when you sit at the board they are foreshortened and appear square. The black stones are slightly larger than the white stones, but by a trick of the eye they appear to be the same size. Even the acoustic properties of the board as you play the stones have been considered."

I swept up a handful of stones and felt them in my hand. Weighty and smooth. "It is a beautiful game."

"It's yours." Sensei smiled. "I'd like to give it to you."

I wanted to thank him, but my eyes were welling up and I had to clamp my lips together. I closed the two wicker baskets, put them on the board and picked it up.

I tried again to thank him, but I was overwhelmed with emotion. He nodded to show that he understood, and we parted ways until the following week.

But the following week he was not there. I sat at the dark-wood table in the old-time pub, bathed in the heat of the fire, feeling self-conscious. The board and the two wicker baskets were laid out in front of me, aching to be played.

As I sat there I realised that I had no way of finding him. I had no idea where he lived, I had none of his contact details – I did not even know his full name.

I waited for him, and when I realised that waiting had become denial, I worried for him. As the worry ran its course I mourned him. I missed him, but there was a more terrible loss pressing at my soul. I feared that I would never again play my perfect game of go.

Just as these notions were devouring my mind, a young man approached me and asked me what the little wicker baskets were for. I looked up, hesitated, shook off my swirling trance of thoughts, and smiled. I opened one of the baskets.

"Are these game pieces?" the young man asked, picking up a stone.

"Yes," I replied.

He indicated the empty chair. "May I join you?"

"Please do," I said, gesturing. "I've been expecting a friend, but he hasn't come."

"What game is it? Maybe I could play."

All at once, I knew what I had to do. "Call me Sensei." I smiled, shaking his hand.

In 2006 my wife and I moved to London and I started a new job. My colleague invited me to join his weekly go club, and taught me how to play (he was a 1 dan player). This story, written in 2007, reflects my deep fascination with the game. It has not been previously published.

THE UNINTENDED CONSEQUENCES OF DRIVERLESS CARS

> 66
>
> *Sharon had to get a job for the first time in her life. Made me feel useless as a condom in a convent.*
>
> 99

I reckon me wife's having an affair.

Sharon and I got together back when I was boning up to be a London cabbie. I was always hunched over a map, or going out for runs on the bike, or sitting there reciting every shopfront from Marylebone to the Old Kent Road. If it weren't for her I'd have forgotten to eat. How she had the patience to stick with me I'll never know.

But I passed the Knowledge in the end, and bought meself a beautiful black TX4. Filled with pride, I was, to be me own boss, to be driving such an iconic symbol of London. We used to call ourselves Cromwell's Army, a nod to 400 years of shared history.

I paid off the cab in three years. After that Sharon and I would take a month off every year and take the kids to Benidorm. That was the life. Sure, I occasionally took a fare that didn't make it onto me tax return, but I was fundamentally an honest cabbie. Not like those bloody Ubers.

That was some time in the 2010s. A seething mass of illiterate immigrants invaded our shores and our incompetent government let them all get jobs as Ubers. Suddenly the roads were flooded with them and good old black taxis were being starved out. I'd half a mind to go to Benidorm and not come back.

We thought we had it bad then, but you know what? It was good to get angry, to have a cause to fight for. We had to work longer hours, but I guess we'd had it easy till then. It felt like we had some power when we coordinated a flash demo on Twitter and brought Zone 1 to a standstill just to make the Mayor sweat. It was uplifting seeing all those taxis turn out, like a long line of worker ants.

Of course, the real hard times were ahead. When Uber announced they were phasing out human beings altogether the death knell was upon us. The protests turned into riots – inevitable with those entitled immigrant crooks joining in – and London burned. I punched an Uber driver or two in Parliament Square, but I regret that. Ultimately, we were on the same side.

Anyway, the riots made sod all difference. Uber put ten thousand driverless minicabs on London's roads every year for five years. I went from being a highly skilled professional, commanding the respect of family and friends, to being on the breadline with the bloody immigrants. Turns out no bugger wanted a professional service, it was all about the cheaper fare. Sharon had to get a job for the first time in her life. Made me feel useless as a condom in a convent.

I kept the cab, and even started taking fares again, doing tours for Yanks and Saudis and Ruskies and Chinese. But I was still feeling sore about the whole thing. It was no surprise when the government passed the Autonomous Vehicles Act, but I refused to get one of those driverless monstrosities no matter how much Sharon begged.

The TX4 drove us everywhere right up until the day manual cars were banned. The first of January 2037 was a sad day for me, knowing she was retired for good. I moved on – became a cop like a lot of ex-cabbies because it was the only way we could still drive a real car – but I still visit the garage every day to admire her graceful curves and keep her polished. I sit in her sometimes and recite twenty-year-old shopfronts from Marylebone to the Old Kent Road.

I bought Sharon a car in the end. A Google Flo SD with alloy wheels and leather seats. I don't use it much, but she loves it. The kids use it too when they're back home. It's ugly as sin as far as I'm concerned, boxy like a camper van in shoulder pads. All the cars are like that now. On the highway they look like Samsonites on an airport baggage carousel. I got in it the other day expecting to sit in the driver's seat, but of course it faces the wrong bloody way – all the seats face inwards.

It was that trip that got me suspicious, actually. About Sharon, I mean. She'd been a bit off with me since we'd got Flo. I didn't know what I'd done wrong, but I wanted to get back in her good books, so I planned a bit of a grand gesture for our anniversary. I was going to buy her a new cycle from the shop she works at. (Sharon was smart taking that cycle mechanic course – what with half of central London pedestrianized now and no cycle deaths for years, it's a booming industry.)

So when Sharon got back from her early shift I made up something about taking the car to the pub for a drink. I jumped in and told Flo, "Last destination, please," expecting to be taken to Brixton Cycles where Sharon worked. It responded with ridiculous cheer – I told it to shut up and spent twenty minutes kicking meself for being so polite to a bloody car.

When I looked up I wasn't at Brixton Cycles at all. I was at that seedy spot round the back of Streatham Common where teenagers go to shag in those rented cars with beds in. Who'd she taken here, I wondered?

It bugged me, but I shrugged it off. At least, until last week. Last week I was on the beat, in me uniform, covering for a mate over Battersea way, when who should I see sneaking around picking up flowers and an expensive looking gift from a boutique on Lavender Hill? Flo – our Flo – the bloody driverless car.

Our anniversary came and went. Sharon liked the cycle, I think. Frankly she wasn't as enthusiastic as she could've been. And there I was, expecting me flowers and me posh pressie, but no. Nothing. So who got them, I asked meself?

This morning I tried to work out where Flo had delivered that gift. I asked the home management system if we'd signed Flo up to Amazon Pool or something, you know, that thing where you let Amazon deliver packages with your car when you're not using it. But the only Amazon service we've got is the fridge. (Can you believe Amazon's doing fridges? Still, haven't run out of Tennent's Super since we got it, so can't complain.)

So then I asked the home management system if it could give me a log of where Flo had been for the last few days. It could. Boom. There it was. Solid evidence that me wife has been up to something. Spending time with someone. Not me.

Here she comes now, back from her shift, or who knows where.

"Evening, love," she said, looking happy as a little girl with an ice cream cone.

I opted to be blunt. "Sharon. Are you having an affair?"

She didn't say anything. Her expression, her hesitation, was more than enough.

"Who's the bloke?" I barked.

"It's not a bloke." She looked like I might hit her.

"What? A bloody woman?"

Her eyes flicked toward the front drive for a split second. I was baffled, the adrenalin pinching at me thoughts, until finally it dawned on me. Me jaw dropped and she kind of shrunk into her shoulders.

"Flo spends time with me," she said. "Takes me places. Listens to me better than you do. And that massage mode, oh . . ."

I didn't know what to say. I spent the rest of the night sitting in me old TX4, caressing the steering wheel, sobbing into a four-pack of Tennent's Super.

First published in Sci Phi Journal

This story is best read aloud in a Cockney accent.

I wrote this in 2015 while I was working in stakeholder relations for the taxi and private hire trade in London. My job included running a Twitter feed to publish regulatory information and help drivers with licensing queries. That was right at the peak of Uber's rowdy disruption of the industry.

I have a huge amount of respect for taxi drivers, but their behaviour on social media was often execrable, and I wrote this story as a gently teasing revenge.

SHIP PSYCHIATRIST

❝

"No, Ancelador," she interrupted. "You tell me. Trust is made whole only when returned."

❞

The room was small. There were two mould chairs, and a table with a drink dispenser and various fidget toys. On the wall, instead of the usual starnet comms panel, hung Ancelador's doctorate in psychiatry from Mare Nebulum University.

He closed the pressure-tight door, and ran his fingers around the frames of the mould chairs, under the table, along the edges of the walls. He searched for several minutes before he was satisfied. As far as he could tell, there were no microphones, no cameras, no comms; no connection at all with the rest of the ship.

"Ship," he commanded. "Captain Stellapluvia. Can you hear me?"

No response.

"Emergency. Hull breach. Loss of cabin pressure. Emergency, emergency. Doctor Ancelador reporting."

No response. Thank goodness. On reflection, that would have been in very bad taste if Stellapluvia had heard it, given the ship's history.

Ancelador was pleased with the therapy room; it was restrained, comfortable, and most importantly private, as he had requested. It needed a few personal touches – a video wall with calming images, some muliebrisoma scent perhaps, ultrasonic music to soothe the patients – but it was an excellent start.

The room tipped, and Ancelador staggered backwards into the door. The ship was accelerating. He pulled himself into one of the mould chairs, which automatically adjusted around him, and waited for the dampers to kick in.

He looked at the empty chair opposite. As ship psychiatrist, he was responsible for the mental wellbeing of the 3,240 men, women, machines and hybrids on board. Which was a joke, because they were all insane or they wouldn't be here. They were all trapped in this graphene bullet of a ship for an indeterminate amount of time, headed for an indeterminate location, clinging to some vague fantasy of frontier colonisation that had an indeterminate chance of success. Only the most broken minds would volunteer themselves for such folly. Not least Ancelador himself.

Ancelador was leaving behind the person he cared most about in the universe. Mvelindor, who had loved him. Mvelindor, who would never forgive him. And now he was giving Mvelindor some space – many light-years of space. Was this bravery or cowardice?

He punched up a light sedative from the drink dispenser and downed it, trying to slow his breathing.

*

After that first day when he'd been shown to his therapy room, it took Ancelador two days to find it again. There were miles of corridors, and he could never seem to find the same room twice. He was tempted to tie a piece of string to a door and unravel it as he went along.

He did find a pool, a music room, a haze room, several themed bars, two mess halls, various sport halls, an impressive holo-library, and the chemical garden. Hard to believe this had once been a warship – it felt more like a pleasure cruiser. It was as if the ship's history had been aggressively erased. At least there was plenty to keep a few thousand wannabe colonists occupied for a few months. Or years.

A chill whipped up Ancelador's spine.

The twelve most senior members of the crew were obliged to book a psychotherapy session once a week – the first appointments were tomorrow. But, so far, no one else had booked, so Ancelador was at leisure. He drifted towards one of the bars, intending to get radically drunk.

The first bar he found was a congress lounge, furnished with beds and harnesses and one-way mirrors. A man and an android were entangled on a plinth, carrying out an impressive feat of sexual athleticism that earned them a smattering of applause from the wasted onlookers. Ancelador thought of Mvelindor, felt sick, and left sharply.

The next bar he found styled itself as an Officers' Club, which was much more his speed. Muted lighting, inoffensive music, bench-style seating. He sat next to a heavily modified human – the man was covered in catlike fur, had cranial implants and tools for fingers.

"Hey, where'd you get that skin?" the man asked. Ancelador was surprised to be asked such a direct question before he'd even settled in his seat.

"Born with it."

"Not an enhancement? That's disappointing. I'd love to get me some skin like that. Never seen anything like it. So black it's blue."

The man had an unusual accent that Ancelador could not place. Ancelador started to punch up a drink, but the man stopped him.

"Wait, try this." The man punched up two neon pink drinks that steamed, like dry ice.

The two of them clinked glasses and drank. It was like inhaling a nuke wrapped in silk. Ancelador tried to say something; nothing came but a tight gasp.

The man laughed, and sipped his own drink. "I'm Refeliodor."

"Refeliodor? You're a senior officer, aren't you?"

"Chief Hyperspace Engineer."

"We have an appointment tomorrow."

"You're the psychiatrist?"

"Ancelador."

Refeliodor laughed again. "Great to meet you."

Ancelador tilted his head. "Hey, you can explain something to me. Now that we have this magical hyperspace engine, can't we just go anywhere we want, like that?" He snapped his fingers.

"The hyperspace drive lets us travel through a higher spatial dimension, but we still have to travel."

"I don't get it."

Refeliodor punched up another pair of pink drinks. He grabbed a napkin, and leaned forward, excited. "Imagine this napkin is our universe, a hundred billion light-years across." His right pinkie had been surgically replaced by a pen; he used it to draw a line from one end of the napkin to the other. "If we could only travel in two dimensions, it would take an unimaginably long time to journey even a fraction of the distance. Even with warp bubbles, faster than light, it would take a billion years."

"Impossible."

"Exactly. But if you can access the next spatial dimension, you realise the universe is actually shaped like this." He crumpled up the napkin into a ball, and pierced his pen-finger through the middle. "Now we can travel right through. On the scale of our napkin, it's still a really long way, but now . . ." He laid the napkin out flat again; it had little holes across it at irregular intervals.

"Every step we take flings us into a new part of the universe."

"Right," Refeliodor grinned. "And from our lower-dimensional perspective it looks like we disappear from one part of space and appear hundreds or millions of light-years away. The problem is, we can't really see the higher dimensions, so it's pretty hard to map. But we can start at our home system, point ourselves in a certain direction on the higher-dimensional axis, and we'll always end up in the same place. And we can come back the same way."

"So we don't know where we're going."

"Well, we don't know where we'll end up, but we know our trajectory. Better still, we can keep secret exactly which way we're going. So, if we find a habitable system, or rare minerals, or alien tech, we'll be able to set up an exclusive trade route."

"*If* we find something. That's a big if."

Refeliodor shrugged. "Space is big."

Which makes it all the more ridiculous that we fought for such a tiny corner of it, thought Ancelador.

*

By the end of his first week on board, Ancelador had counselled all the senior officers, and a handful of other passengers. Most had typical mental hang-ups. Depression, anxiety, corporeal detachment disorder, digital dissociative disorder, post-traumatic stress, space shrink. Unsurprisingly, the ruinous war still clouded their souls.

The Chief of Security had the worst case of corporeal detachment disorder he had ever seen. Ancelador was baffled how many people transferred their consciousnesses into android bodies without considering the psychological consequences. This poor guy was suffering everything from phantom limb pain to severe asomatognosia. At least, now that he had an ageless body, he had a few hundred years to work it out.

Refeliodor, the Chief Hyperspace Engineer, seemed to be the only sane one among them. Ancelador couldn't help but suspect he was hiding something. But the man was so damn personable he hadn't yet managed to dig any deeper.

The one senior crew member Ancelador had not yet seen was the captain herself, Stellapluvia. He waited for her in his therapy room, wringing his fingers. Her legend preceded her; but he must not allow his curiosity to distract his professional judgment.

She had led the Doradus System's greatest fleet to victory, against impossible odds. In this very ship. A devastatingly expensive victory, so many hundreds of thousands of lives and minds lost, but she had done it. Landed on the Melnick fortress planet, and stolen the secret of hyperspace technology. She had been two people then, the woman Stellador, and the ship's mind Pluvia Ignis. When the Melnicks surrendered, she returned as a single amalgamated consciousness – a new mind in Stellador's body.

She had returned augmented, but somehow damaged. She had spurned publicity, refused medals and honours, become a recluse; and ended up here – captaining the shell of the Pluvia Ignis into unknown deep space. What had happened to her on that fortress planet?

The pressure-tight door opened, making Ancelador jump.

"Oh, you startled –"

The rest of his words disappeared. He smelled her at the same time he saw her. A heady scent, pine, musk, like a rainswept Doradan ever-forest. Like home. She wore a traditional rock-wrap with a thick scarf that hid half her face, emphasising her chilling sea-green eyes. Across her left cheekbone, a ragged scar that intimated a thousand stories. Ancelador wanted to run his thumb along it and tell her everything would be ok.

Those eyes. They analysed Ancelador with ruthless efficiency; a dozen saccades, and he felt as if his deepest self had been exposed. Those arctic eyes gave nothing away, and he reminded himself he was dealing with a sophisticated military intellect. Her mind was both human and machine; combined, enhanced, doubled.

"Captain Stellapluvia," said Ancelador. "Welcome."

She shut the door behind her and walked into the room. Ancelador gathered himself and sat in one of the mould chairs, gesturing to Stellapluvia to sit in the other. She did so, precisely, sparely.

There was silence between them for some moments. Ancelador wore his warmest expression, professional empathy, inviting her to feel at ease and talk when she was ready. Her expression was inscrutable, half-hidden by the thick scarf.

He sensed she would not talk first. He sensed his usual approach would not work here. She would not respond to the subtle emotional manipulations he employed, with infinite gentleness, to tease out even the most bitterly guarded secrets. He needed a more direct approach. She was smarter than him, and they both knew it.

Ancelador's expression hardened. "Thank you for providing me with a truly private room," he said. "Confidentiality is paramount."

"Essential." Her voice was shockingly small. Almost meek. "But very hard to guarantee."

With calculated deliberation, she unwrapped her scarf. As each layer unwound, she was revealed. Her chiselled nose. Her pale lips. Her fragile neck. She bundled the scarf in her lap in a curiously childish way, and leaned forward with an earnestness that made Ancelador's heart skip – awe, or panic, he could not tell.

She spoke again. "Why are you here, Dr Ancelador? What are you running from?"

Mvelindor's face appeared unbidden in Ancelador's consciousness. He controlled his expression, swallowed the bile that had risen in his throat. "These sessions are not about me, Captain."

"Who counsels the counsellor?"

Ancelador bit the inside of his cheek. "We –" he hesitated. How did she provoke him so easily? "The war was hard on all of us."

She sat back. Nodded. She had been open, but now, suddenly, her wall was up again. Ancelador was just beginning to process the situation, and she had already reached her conclusion. He felt dizzy.

She hastily wrapped the scarf back around her face. "I believe you've met the Chief Hyperspace Engineer. Have a look at his personnel file before you see him again."

And she left.

Ancelador stared at the door from which she had just departed, trying to make sense of what had happened. What had she said? Confidentiality was hard to guarantee? Why had she wanted to know about him? Was it a defence mechanism? Did she somehow already know his terrible secret? But how could she? And why mention Refeliodor?

He felt lost, utterly outgunned.

He slept fitfully that night, running over the brief conversation in his head, again and again.

*

Ancelador met Refeliodor in the Officers' Club every evening. They chatted like old friends, about their likes and dislikes, about ship's gossip, about space, about work, about how they were keeping themselves entertained on the ship. But, he noticed, never about the past. That would have to wait for the therapy room.

At the back of his mind was Stellapluvia's bizarre suggestion to look at Refeliodor's personnel file. For days, he resisted. But when it was nearly time for their weekly psychotherapy session, he found a quiet corner of the holo-library and read through all of the senior officers' files.

He read Stellapluvia's file with particular interest. Stellador was born on Arcadia, the fourth Doradan planet. She had distinguished herself at an early age in the protracted Magellanic War, years before Ancelador was even born. She had advised on the construction of the Pluvia Ignis, the first of a new class of warship designed for speed and stealth. The Pluvia Ignis was endowed with a cutting-edge machine intelligence, and when its sentience had achieved self-potentiation, it had selected Stellador as its human captain. Together they had fought in several notable battles, ultimately being promoted to General Ovidor's second-in-command. Their final battle was for the Melnick fortress planet, about which the file's information was brief and bland: The battle was a Doradan victory. The Pluvia Ignis had been partially destroyed, and its consciousness had been merged with Stellador's. The rest of the file was redacted, marked "Captain's eyes only".

Ancelador saved Refeliodor's file for last. But when he looked, he found nothing. He searched again, convinced he had missed something, but Refeliodor simply had no personnel file. He was listed on the crew roster as "Chief Hyperspace Engineer", but there was none of the usual biographical information – it was as if the entire file had been redacted.

Ancelador closed the files, and chewed a fingernail.

Later that day, his therapy session with Refeliodor started straightforwardly enough. Refeliodor bustled into the room and they greeted each other by pressing foreheads together – Refeliodor's catlike fur felt pleasant against Ancelador's skin.

"Hey, doc," grinned Refeliodor, plunging into the mould chair. He opened with a characteristically direct question, in his unplaceable accent. "How the hell do you do your job, anyway?"

Ancelador sat down. "What do you mean?"

"Like, someone sits down here, and they're clearly not right in the head, although they'll deny it to their grave. What do you do about it?"

"Support, scrutinise, scramble, section."

"What?"

"There are four approaches to psychotherapy," Ancelador explained. "Support, which is giving someone the tools to look after themselves, teaching them resilience, building self-esteem, and so on. Scrutinise, which is to dig into their past to better understand whatever may have damaged them, and face it head-on. Scramble, which is to fill them with drugs."

"And section, which is to give up on them entirely."

Ancelador made a non-committal grunt.

Refeliodor laughed. "I like the sound of scramble."

"Most people don't need any help with that one."

"Well, what are we doing today, doc? Support or scrutinise?"

"That's up to you, Refeliodor. Although, there is one thing I would like to ask you, if I may."

"Of course."

"Why is your personnel file blank?"

Refeliodor's bright expression didn't change, but suddenly he was making an effort to maintain it. "That's something I've been meaning to talk to you about, Ancelador, since we've become friends. This conversation is confidential, correct?"

"Absolutely."

"My name's not really Refeliodor." A moment's hesitation, but only a moment. "It's Din-har Ix Habiyan Taranto À."

"You're Melnick?" Ancelador realised he had failed to control his expression, and tried to neutralise it, but knew it was too late, and so let his sincere reaction play out.

"Yes."

"How –" Ancelador started, but cut himself short.

"Hyperspace tech is entirely new to the Doradus System. No Doradans have sufficient expertise. I was asked to join the crew. Without me, your hyperspace drive would be extremely dangerous. At least until the rest of the engineers get up to speed."

That explained his quirky accent – it was not native, but learned. Ancelador closed his jaw. "I can understand why you're being discreet about your background. There are people out there who would lynch you."

Refeliodor sighed. "Melnick civilisation is, unfortunately, often misunderstood in the Doradan culture."

"Thank you for trusting me."

Refeliodor brightened up again. "It's a pleasure to be able to talk to someone."

For the next hour, Refeliodor spoke animatedly about his home planet. Ancelador had believed himself smart enough to know that the endless anti-Melnick propaganda was exaggerated, but one by one, the veil was drawn away from his unconscious prejudices. Refeliodor painted a picture of the Melnicks as compassionate, cultured, innovating, wise. Ancelador could feel their passion for understanding, their pride in their achievements, their love for their home system.

The session ended all too quickly, and Ancelador regretted that the next time he saw Refeliodor, they would not be able to talk freely. They touched foreheads affectionately.

"Thank you," Refeliodor said, as he left Ancelador alone in the room.

*

The next day was his second weekly session with Stellapluvia. As he waited for her to arrive, Ancelador's heartbeat betrayed him. He could not calm himself. He tried to self-analyse – what was he feeling?

Dread. What was it about this woman that triggered him so?

She entered and sat without ceremony. Her scent, her eyes, her clockwork energy – Ancelador closed his eyes for a moment and forced himself to focus.

"Good afternoon, Captain," he said.

"Dr Ancelador."

"Thank you for making time for me. It's very important, I believe, to make time to talk. Do you agree?"

She did not respond, only looked at him, unwavering, half her face hidden behind the thick scarf.

"This is a safe space," he said, reassuring. "There's nothing right or wrong you can say. Anything you do say will be kept in the strictest confidence."

She remained silent.

"Perhaps you'd like to talk about how you came to be on this ship?" It was the perfect question – he'd prepared it in advance. It was intentionally ambiguous; she could take it to mean how she ended up on this mission, or she could talk about her more distant past, when she'd been both a woman and a machine mind.

But she did neither. "We're being followed," she said.

"What?" blurted Ancelador. He had heard her clearly, despite her diminutive voice, but what she said was so unexpected he needed to hear it again.

"We're being followed. This information must not leave this room. The Chief of Security reported a heat signature last week, and it's trailing us. Almost certainly a cloaked ship. But it shouldn't be possible. Our bearing is highly confidential. The only explanation is that somebody on board leaked it. A traitor."

So much at once. Ancelador waited for his words to catch up with his brain. "W-why are you telling me?"

"Only three people on this ship know our bearing. Me, the Chief Navigator, and the Chief Hyperspace Engineer. You already know whom I suspect. You have . . . unusual access to him. See what you can find out."

"But . . ."

"Show me what you're made of, Dr Ancelador." She nodded without breaking eye contact, then got up and left.

Had she really just asked him to spy on Refeliodor? Several minutes passed before Ancelador trusted himself to stand.

*

The nights with Refeliodor in the Officers' Club did not flow as freely as they had done before. Ancelador felt guilty. He was worried that Refeliodor would assume Ancelador's prejudices against Melnicks had tainted their relationship. Nevertheless, after a few days, Ancelador avoided the Officers' Club, preferring to spend time alone, trying to work through his mixed feelings.

Closer and closer crept the time when he would see Refeliodor in the therapy room again for the weekly appointment – and the day after, Stellapluvia. For the first, he could hardly wait. The second filled him with angst.

Could Refeliodor be a traitor? Had Ancelador been so naïve, to be transported by Refeliodor's halcyon description of his home world? Refeliodor wasn't even the man's real name. But he was a friend, Ancelador trusted him, felt it in his bones – *wanted* to feel it, but did he feel it, really? And what did it mean that the ship was being followed? By whom? With what intent? Why had Captain Stellapluvia burdened him with that frightening knowledge? What did she expect of him? He was terrified of disappointing her. Ancelador's internal world stormed so violently that, by comparison, the content of his days seemed insipid, irrelevant.

At last, the day came. Ancelador arrived in the therapy room an hour early for Refeliodor's appointment. He was so agitated, he found himself unable to call on any of his self-calming techniques. He resorted to playing frantically with the fidget toys.

When Refeliodor arrived, Ancelador did not hide his emotion. He leapt out of his seat and hugged the man, then stepped back, professionally embarrassed. Refeliodor had not returned the hug.

The two men sat awkwardly. Refeliodor made brief eye contact, then looked at the floor. "I'm glad for the hearty greeting, friend."

"I'm . . ." Ancelador floundered. "Usually, I must control my emotions inside the therapy room, and be free outside. I'm not used to it being the other way around."

"I thought you might hate me. I deserve it."

"No." Ancelador was earnest. "You had no choice, you had to withhold the truth about your background – no hard feelings."

"You don't understand. There's more."

Ancelador tried to say something tactful, encouraging, but it stuck unformed in his throat.

Refeliodor held his furry head in his hands. "I've been going round and round in my head, angry at myself for having accepted this assignment. I believed it would be some kind of atonement – but I'm a charlatan. If I have to pretend to be someone else, how can my apology be sincere? How can my forgiveness?"

Ancelador trod carefully. "Forgiveness . . . for what?"

Refeliodor did not answer immediately. He seemed to be trying to control his breathing. "We were at war."

Ancelador swallowed hard. "Yes. That's part of us. But we can choose what to make of it."

"You've got to see it from our perspective. We never wanted to fight. We were happy in our little sector of the Magellanic Cloud. But the Doradans wouldn't leave us alone. Your politicians, your General Ovidor, wanted our worlds, our technology. We would happily have shared, but you were intent on conquest. Not you, I mean, sorry, but . . ."

"Go on," coaxed Ancelador.

"A show of force. That's what was planned. The only language the Doradans would understand. We found a planet in the Melnick Sector that we could reach with our hyperspace drive, and we led you to it."

"The fortress planet."

"But it was a trap. You arrived with your fleet, assuming you had us outnumbered." He trailed off.

Ancelador was silent, trying to understand the implications.

Refeliodor looked up, his eyes wet. "I'm sorry. It was me. I suggested the whole despicable plan. And then so many of your people were killed."

Ancelador felt strangely calm. "We knew," he said.

"What? You knew the fortress planet was a decoy?"

"No." he admitted. "But we knew it was a trap. We knew our forces would be decimated. There was glory in fighting anyway. I was a fleet psychiatrist, clearing thousands of soldiers as mentally fit for combat. I knew I was sending most of them to their deaths. They knew it too."

"Then . . . why . . ."

"It's part of who we are, Refeliodor. And now we can choose what to make of it."

Refeliodor sighed. "Now I'm stuck on this ship. When I volunteered, I thought there was something poetic about serving on the ship that had led my enemy in battle. It felt pleasingly . . . circular. A karmic route to redemption."

"And now?"

"And now, I don't know. Maybe this is apt penance, or maybe it's just another thoughtless waste."

"You feel guilty."

Refeliodor did not respond, his eyes downcast. Ancelador left him to his thoughts, trying not to let his own distract him. But he could not help feeling angry at Refeliodor, or whatever his name was. He dared claim responsibility for a hundred thousand Doradan deaths?

Ancelador closed his eyes for a moment, reminding himself of his job. He was psychiatrist, not judge. He should feel pity, not rage. He liked Refeliodor. Refeliodor was a good person. He felt it intuitively – yet he doubted it. The two opposing judgments roiled in his gut, failing to reconcile, like water and oil.

Captain Stellapluvia's warning resurfaced in Ancelador's mind. What else might Refeliodor feel guilty about? What else was he holding back?

Ancelador put on his mask of professional empathy. "Please, keep talking. Tell me everything that's on your mind."

*

Ancelador cancelled the rest of his appointments that day, feigning sickness. He stayed in his therapy room, alone, mashing one of the fidget toys. He punched up a light sedative, but did not drink it, wishing to keep a clear head.

He was ashamed that he had allowed a patient to make him so emotional. He tried to detach himself. He reminded himself that Refeliodor was an engineer, not a general. The man could have no more responsibility for the battle than Ancelador himself had by clearing soldiers as fit for combat. Refeliodor was as broken as any of them aboard this ship, and deserved the same comradeship and care.

But something remained in Ancelador's mind like a splinter. Something was not right about Refeliodor. About what he'd said. Ancelador knew he must put those feelings aside if he wanted to continue his relationship with Refeliodor, whether as psychiatrist or friend. But the feeling would not be denied.

That night, his dreams plumbed morbid depths. But it was not Refeliodor that his imagination conjured, nor Stellapluvia. Instead, his troubled thoughts expressed themselves in the face of Mvelindor. Mvelindor, who had loved him. Mvelindor, who would never forgive him. Mvelindor appeared, not righteously angry, but crushingly disappointed.

Ancelador woke feeling exhausted. One by one, all his troubled thoughts re-entered his mind. His friend, Refeliodor, was not whom he seemed. The ship's trajectory had been betrayed. Captain Stellapluvia wanted Ancelador to act the spy. And she was coming to see him today.

He conducted his morning appointments mechanically, trying so hard not to think about his troubles, that all he could do was think about his troubles. Before he was ready, Captain Stellapluvia was at his door.

"You're early," said Ancelador.

Captain Stellapluvia closed the door behind her and sat. Her intoxicating smell. Her baleful eyes. The storied scar on her cheek. Her expression was unreadable, obscured by her scarf. "The situation has escalated," she said, with disquieting mildness.

"Situation?"

"The ship pursuing us is armed and dangerous. I need information, Dr Ancelador. Did you question the Chief Hyperspace Engineer?" Her eyes never broke contact. Once again, Ancelador was derailed by her pace, her bluntness.

"He told me everything," he said, before he'd had a chance to leaven his response.

"And what did you discover?"

The splinter itched in Ancelador's mind. But which was greater, his duty to his captain, or his duty to his patient? He attempted a deflection, but it was weak. "Captain Stellapluvia, we're not here to talk about Refeliodor. We're here to talk about you."

"You know something important," she said. "I can see it in your face."

Ancelador touched his face, and immediately scolded himself – how did this woman so effortlessly upset his balance? He felt an irresistible compulsion to confess all to Stellapluvia. The turbulence of his thoughts had been causing him sleepless nights and wakeless days. He needed to talk to someone, and here was the one person on the ship that could undoubtedly read people better than him. She, alone in the universe, could help him. She had said it herself. Who counsels the counsellor?

"Refeliodor is . . ." he started – but then he thought of Mvelindor. The last and only time he had abused the trust invested in him.

No. Not again.

He put his hand to his mouth, needing the physical pressure to stop himself from talking.

Stellapluvia's malevolent eyes sparkled. "You have to tell me. Damn your professional confidentiality. This is an existential threat."

Ancelador's hand remained over his mouth.

"If you don't tell me what you know," she admonished, "you are answerable for the consequences. Your secrets will be useless when we're both dead."

There was a terrible silence between them. Wars were won and lost. Civilisations grew and fell. Stars coalesced and fulminated. Ancelador shook his head. He would not make the same mistake.

"No," he said, his voice cracking.

He felt sure the captain would leave, and he'd be disgraced. Or worse. But she stayed. Her gaze did not waver, though her intensity ebbed.

Slowly, she unwrapped her scarf. Her lips were thin. Her bone structure angular. Her neck gangly. Brittle.

She bundled the scarf on her lap. Twirled a tassel around her finger.

One corner of her lips twisted. "Forgive my deception."

"W-what?"

"We're not being chased."

"Oh." Ancelador tried to process this. "And . . . Refeliodor?" he asked.

"I don't know what he told you. I don't want to know. But he can be trusted. I selected him for my crew, personally."

"You were testing me."

She nodded. "Confidentiality is hard to guarantee."

Only when his muscles relaxed did Ancelador realise how tense they had been. He leaned back in his chair, feeling weary. He was astonished at how childlike and unthreatening Stellapluvia suddenly appeared. Her posture was softer. Her eyes unfocussed, as if she was lost in thought.

"General Ovidor knew it was a suicide mission," she said.

Ancelador felt a beatific serenity, safe as a womb.

She continued. "He asked me to lead hundreds of thousands of loyal soldiers to their deaths."

"It was impossible. How did you get through?" he asked, indulging his curiosity. "How did you make it onto the fortress planet?"

Stellapluvia shook her head. "We didn't win the war. We lost. It was a devastating defeat. I spent hundreds of thousands of lives to crash-land on that planet, and it was barren."

"It was a decoy," Ancelador said, matter-of-fact.

Ancelador was shocked to see tears running from her eyes. "They baited us to a system that they could reach with their hyperspace drive. We thought we were fighting an army, but we were fighting an empire. They kept appearing, out of nowhere. Blinking into existence and blasting us to pieces. The Pluvia Ignis was hit. We crash landed on the fortress planet. The ship's mind was badly damaged. The only way I could save it was to merge with it. It was unconscionably painful. The ship's mind had been dying, and suddenly we were combined – it was the most existentially terrifying disorientation. It was like becoming a savant with brain damage."

Ancelador realised what had been bothering him. The splinter in his mind. "But you were victorious. If the planet was barren, how did you steal the hyperspace drive?"

"The Melnicks didn't surrender, that's propaganda. We surrendered. In secret, we signed a peace treaty. Basically, they gave us hyperspace technology, and we promised to leave them alone. They were happy to give us the tech if it meant we took our dreams of conquest as far away from them as possible. Then, to make sure we couldn't abuse our advantage, they offered the same treaty to every other faction in the Magellanic Cloud. We ended the Magellanic War – not by winning, but by sacrificing ourselves."

Ancelador leaned forward. "You carry a heavy burden."

Stellapluvia locked eyes with him again, and he felt molten. "As do we all," she said.

"Tell me –"

"No, Ancelador," she interrupted. "You tell me. Trust is made whole only when returned."

"I – I . . . served in that battle," he said, hesitating. He could not possibly give voice to his greatest shame, yet he knew he must. He felt disembodied as he spoke. "I was doing psychiatric evaluations, declaring them fit for combat, on the unspoken understanding that everyone was to be declared fit for combat. The best I could do was to help these men and women and machines prepare themselves. Accept their fate. Thousands upon thousands being sent to their deaths."

"That must have been difficult for you," soothed Stellapluvia.

"There was only one person I declared unfit. My beloved Mvelindor. He was sent to an asylum. He'll never forgive me. I thought it better for him to hate me and live, than love me and die."

Stellapluvia put her hand on his, and he broke down into tears. Crying, with abandon, for the first time since he'd banished his sweet Mvelindor. He did not stop for several minutes, and even when he could have stopped, he let his feelings flow out, gratefully.

Stellapluvia's voice was comfortingly quiet. "Now we're bound by each other's secrets. Each of us the counsellor, each of us the counselled."

Ancelador wiped his nose on his sleeve. "Thank you, Captain."

That evening, Ancelador sought out Refeliodor. The two of them drank and talked and laughed until the small hours of the morning, as if they had been childhood friends.

After a year of writer's drought, brought on in part by the upheaval of the Covid-19 pandemic, two things inspired me to write this story in the autumn of 2021.

First, an ultra-creative friend started writing a story based on a science fiction universe created by a buddy of his. He shared the rules and parameters of this universe with me, and I took it as a challenge.

Second, my dad found a diary written by his dad in 1967, when he was ship doctor on the last transatlantic voyage of the famous ocean liner RMS Queen Mary. I knew my Gramps as an eccentric old man who ate only smoked salmon sandwiches and wore a tie to ski, so I was fascinated to read this glimpse into his younger self. It made me want to write a story about a ship psychiatrist – or, rather, a spaceship psychiatrist.

BAGGIO'S STORY

"

I have subjugated myself to a dolt.

"

I would like to be a philosopher.

Well, anyone who has used the word "why" can argue that he is a philosopher. I want to be more than that. I want to be *remembered* as a philosopher.

One day I will be dead. People will look back at my life, and they might say I was a martial artist, for I have earned a seventh-dan black belt (in both karate and judo). They might say I was a musician, for I have composed successful operas (in three different languages). They might say I was a footballer, for I used to represent Italy (and scored twenty-seven goals for my country during my career).

But above all, they will say, he was a great philosopher.

The difference between a hobby and greatness is total immersion, to the sacrifice of all else. I must devote my entire life to this pursuit; I must give up absolutely everything for this cause.

I assumed that giving up my material wealth would be the easiest part of this quest, but it is proving not to be straightforward.

Yesterday, I hired a removal van and packed it with all my possessions, leaving my house utterly bare. I drove out to the public common and unpacked the van, laying every item out upon the grass.

I labelled my bank cards with the relevant PIN numbers. I labelled my bicycle lock with its code. I labelled my house keys with their address, and my car keys with instructions for finding the car. I abandoned the rented van, for liabilities are also proprietary.

Finally, I stripped the clothes off my back and folded them into a neat pile. And I walked away.

It was late by then, and cold. I decided to defer the next part of my mission until the morning. So I wandered the streets, looking for a warm place to sleep for a few hours.

No haven was forthcoming. The few warm corners I did find were barred to me by people who I suppose took issue with my nakedness.

I ended up walking aimlessly all night, to keep from freezing. As the sun rose and the pre-dawn chill passed, I found myself approaching the common again – my subconscious mind had guided me in a large circle back to where I started. The soft, dewy grass soothed my aching feet.

I walked up to the pile of my belongings. There were a few people staring at it as they passed, mostly early-morning joggers and peripatetic tramps.

Not a single item was missing.

Ashamed as I am to admit it, my first reaction was to feel hurt that nobody had valued my possessions enough to claim them; but of course I did not indulge my misplaced pride.

I waved down a passing cyclist and asked him why he had not stopped to take something.

"This stuff is yours?" he asked.

"Not any more," I replied. "I wish to give it all away. Would you like to take something? Perhaps this stylish Armani duffle coat? It is a cold morning, after all."

He looked at me, and then glanced all around him as if looking for a candid camera. "No thanks." He frowned, and cycled away.

I noticed a vagrant inspecting the pile of goods, and I approached him. "Would you like some help carrying a few items away?" I asked.

"Jumble sale, is it?" he mumbled, his eyes still ranging over the assortment of household wares.

"If you like," I remarked, "except that every item is free of charge."

"Just looking," he grunted.

I mentally shrugged my shoulders and prepared to walk away, but an irresistible impulse to see the job through to completion compelled me to do one more thing.

I walked over to my writing desk, which was on the grass between my mixing deck and my unicycle, and I pulled a bullet-tip pen out of the top drawer.

I carried over a large imitation Caravaggio I had knocked off during primary school (perfect in every detail, of course), and propped it against the desk so that the back of the frame was facing outwards. I wrote across the wood in bold lettering: "EVERYTHING FREE. HELP YOURSELF."

"Excuse me, sir," came a voice from behind me. I capped the pen and turned around. It was a policeman. "Is that your van, sir?"

"No," I said, looking over to where the rented van was parked.

He sensed he would have to be more specific. "Did you rent that van, sir?"

"Yes."

"It's illegally parked, sir, you'll have to move it at once." The policeman surveyed the pile of personal property laid out on the ground in front of us and his brow creased. "Are these things yours, sir?"

"No."

"They are your things, sir. Look, this golf bag has your name on it. You're that footballer – played for Italy, didn't you?"

"I am a philosopher," I retorted.

"I'm afraid you can't leave these things here, sir."

"They're not my things any more. I've given them away."

"Regardless, sir, you can't leave 'em here."

"I will leave them here. You'll have to arrest me."

"I'm not going to arrest you, sir, although I will insist that you put some clothes on and pack these things back into your van."

With frustration, I intercepted an attractive young woman who was pushing two children in a pram. "Excuse me, madam." I smiled. "Can I interest you in a proposition?"

The woman stopped and eyed me with suspicion. I continued: "I would like to give you everything I own, and in return all I ask is that you take responsibility for it. You see, this policeman here insists that I must move it all away, but I don't want anything to do with it."

"Don't be silly," admonished the woman.

"But these commodities are worth hundreds of thousands of pounds!" I appealed.

The woman cocked her head and scratched her chin. She surveyed the paraphernalia on offer, and her brow furrowed as if conducting a challenging mental calculation. At last, after a full minute, she spoke: "I'll give you ten grand for the lot."

I sighed. I might even have rolled my eyes. "You can have it for free," I clarified. "All of it."

"Well, if you're gonna play hardball, no deal," she huffed, and stomped away.

I turned back to the policeman with an exasperated look. He glared at me as if he were a teacher expecting an apology from a naughty pupil. "Well," I said, "if you're not going to arrest me . . ." And I walked away.

My attention turned fully to the task at hand. The path to greatness is total sacrifice. To be a philosopher, all I need is my mind and a pen. Everything else must go.

I intend to make the ultimate living sacrifice: I will give away my free will.

With no distractions, I will achieve a purity of mind more complete than anyone has achieved before me. And the consequences of my sacrifice will be the subject of my study.

Then I will be, above all, a philosopher.

*

It has now been three days since I gave away my free will and my experiment is not going well.

Before I decided to relinquish my freedom, part of me was concerned about the degradation and humiliation to which I would be exposing myself, for if I was commanded to do housework in a bikini for the rest of my waking life, I would do it. That is a natural risk of devolving my decision-making.

And another part of me hoped with eternal optimism that, unfettered by laziness or lack of self-belief, I would be able to reach my full potential, for if I was commanded to colonise the moon I would devote every fibre of my being to that purpose until it was achieved. That is the divine potential of forgoing free will.

These extremes of possibility excited me. And I felt certain that whatever happened, I would be inspired by the insights into the human psyche that this noble pursuit would provide.

However, I find myself neither in heaven nor hell, but a cramped and lifeless purgatory.

I gave away my free will at random so my ego would not contaminate the decision. I asked each passer-by if he or she would accept responsibility for my decisions until one of them said yes.

After many rejections, a tall, dark-haired, smiling man stopped to consider my proposal. To protect his identity, I will call him Leo.

"So I'd make all your decisions," Leo confirmed. "I could make you do whatever I wanted? Even —"

"Yes, even that," I interrupted. "The lone exception is that I reserve the right to make one recurring decision: While you're asleep I may choose to muse and write, for I wish to be remembered as a philosopher."

"What do you expect me to decide to do with your life?" he asked. "What if I mess it up, or waste it?"

"You can do whatever you want. It's not my place to say. Even if you feel like you're wasting my life you'll be doing me a great service, for by taking away my responsibility for making decisions, you're freeing my mind to think more clearly and deeply than ever before."

"For how long?"

"If you accept, that is not for me to decide."

He asked a number of practical questions such as where I would live and how I would eat, and each time I replied with a similar answer. It would all be up to him.

"It's quite a responsibility," he said at last. He surveyed me with considerable curiosity.

"It is likely to be a significant commitment of time and effort," I admitted. "But I have no expectations, so you have no responsibility to me in that sense. If you desire payment, you can make me work for you in whatever way you want."

"Well, if I can make you decide any time to take back responsibility for your own decisions, then it's zero risk for me . . . I have just one more question."

"Yes?"

"If I told you to, would you kill yourself?"

"Without hesitation."

"I'm in."

He took me back to his home, a claustrophobic one-bedroom flat in a converted Victorian terrace. The place was tidy enough, but structurally questionable. The fading patterned wallpaper had the occasional inexplicable dent or damp patch in it.

He briefly showed me around and then gave me some instructions.

"Right," he asserted. "If you're hungry, you're to eat bread. If you're thirsty, you're to drink water. If you need the toilet, go. If you're tired, sleep. If there's danger, you must get away from it. Those basic rules last forever, and take priority over any other decisions I make for you, unless I specifically override them. Do you understand?"

"Yes," I nodded. Inwardly, I felt pleased that he seemed to have grasped his new role quickly and with intelligence.

"Excellent." Leo smiled. "I'm late for work now. Stay in here and watch TV till I get back."

"What channel?" I asked.

"Channel one," he ordered, and turned to leave, bolting the door behind him.

For nine hours I obeyed, absorbing inane daywatch with all its empty rhetoric.

I felt a frisson of excitement when I heard him come back in – now the game would really begin. But I was to be sadly disappointed.

His opening words were: "I thought you might've tried to steal everything." I shook my head in response. "You're serious about this, then?" he asked, without needing an answer.

Then he set about his evening rituals, barely acknowledging me at all. I had not been given any other decision beyond watching television, so I continued to watch as he showered, ironed his shirts, prepared supper, called his mother . . .

He gave me a portion of food and told me to eat it, and three hours later he went to bed. That was it. No scintillating conversational exchanges. No deep analysis of the potential of my sacrifice. No bizarre or daring decisions. No imagination whatsoever.

Time passed until I felt I could safely assume he was asleep, but I was too discouraged, too brainwashed by hours of dullness, to take up a pen and begin my philosophical musings. So I tried, unsuccessfully, to sleep.

The next day, yesterday, I hoped for better things. But the same tedious scene was played out; and again today.

I have subjugated myself to a dolt.

I am this man's puppet, yet he plays me with no imagination, no art. Without imagination, a puppet is an empty thing, but with imagination, all the world's a stage. If only he used me with a bit more creativity, then we could achieve powerful things.

Even if he abused me I'd prefer it, provided he showed a little flair.

But it is clear that this man will not catalyse my mission. He is incapable. Now I must focus on training my mind to think more deeply, so that it doesn't matter what my body is doing. I must start writing my philosophical masterpiece.

He is asleep now, and the pen is in my hand.

*

Six months have passed, and my life has changed forever. All concern I ever had for the direction and meaning of my life has faded away. My past achievements mean nothing to me any more. Even my philosophical opus, although I still think about it sometimes, has fallen by the wayside.

And I'm happier than I've ever been.

My master, Leo, is wiser and more cunning than I suspected. Those first few days of dullness were merely his way of helping me to appreciate the consequences of being a creature without free will. I laugh at myself now for having been so arrogant.

On the eighth day – it feels so long ago now – I confronted him. He had just returned from work and started his usual routine (I was watching television of course), when I blurted out: "I'm bored!"

"Then decide to be happy," he ordered.

"But how can I? You've been given an opportunity that is unique in the history of humankind and you're too much of an imbecile to do anything with it."

He raised his eyebrows, and let a silence hang in the air for a moment. "Did you just *decide* to say that? To insult me? Did you decide off your own bat?"

"No," I objected, "I've been bursting to say it for days and I was no longer able to hold back."

"Fine. Keep watching television."

"But what will that achieve?"

"You tell me," he countered. "You're the one who gave up your free will."

"Yes, but –"

"But what?" he interrupted, splaying his arms in the air. This was the most animated I'd seen him. "You told me it didn't matter if I wasted your life. You told me I had no responsibility to achieve anything with you. So, tell me, why are you doing this?"

"I gave away my need to make decisions so I could focus more of my mind on deeper thoughts," I explained.

"You're so full of yourself! Can't you see how ridiculous that is?"

"I'm a greater person than you'll ever be!" I yelled.

"Really? What makes you so great?" he shouted back.

"I have the achievements of several lifetimes behind me, and you still live in a crappy flat and call your mother every day!"

"Well, now I control you, so you're only as great as me. If you don't like that, then leave! Every day I come back from work and I expect you not to be here, because you've given up – because you've decided to make your own decisions again and get out of here. *Why are you still here?*"

He had started pacing around in front of me as he said this, like a buzzing mosquito. I felt disproportionately annoyed at him, and I was determined to swat him away. "If you want me to leave, tell me to leave. Tell me to choose another master."

"Why should I? It makes no odds to me."

"Well then, leave me alone, so I can get on with my thinking. Your shallow little brain is sapping my thoughts away."

"You're full of crap. Show me one deep thought you've written since you've been here."

"I've not yet committed anything to paper."

"Then *tell* me one deep thought you've come up with since being here."

"No!" I whined.

"Ha! A-*ha*! That's not your decision to make," he asserted, with some degree of glee. "I'm deciding that you *will* tell me all of your deepest thoughts."

"I –" I started, but then I realised that I had to comply. I had no free will, and I had been given a direct order, so I had to comply.

I opened my mouth, ready to dispense some searing piece of wisdom that would quieten him at last, but with a horrible sinking feeling in my stomach, I realised that I could not think of anything at all.

The sinking feeling grew into a mental panic. That was the turning point: I realised that I had not had a single deep thought since the day I gave away everything I owned at the public common.

I had not written a word of philosophy since this experiment began. And it was my own fault, not Leo's. That single revelation, the possibility that I was failing because *I* was inadequate, terrified me to the core. I stayed silent.

"There you go," Leo said calmly. "Now watch television and think about what you've done. Think about what you want. I'm going to bed."

As he left he added: "If you're not here in the morning, goodbye."

But I stayed. I was too shaken to move on. I didn't even have anywhere to go – and now I could see that I might have given it all away for nothing. Had I ever had a deep thought in my life? The more I thought about it the more it scared me. I was all success and no soul.

I watched television all night, numbing my brain to the emptiness of my situation. Leo did not say a word to me in the morning as he got up and left for work.

I cried. I wasn't even sure what for.

I had to think. Leo had ordered me to think about what I wanted. Without really being conscious that I was making a decision to do so, I left the flat and went for a walk.

I inhaled the crisp sunshine air as I approached the common. I cast my eyes over the scattered people jogging, walking, chatting, sitting; and I asked myself, "Why?"

Why was I here? Why had I done all the things I had done? Why was I unhappy?

I was back in the flat when Leo returned from work. The television was off.

"How are you feeling?" asked Leo.

"Lost," I admitted. "I would like to stay, if I may."

"Sure." He nodded sympathetically. He studied me for a while, and I think the corners of his mouth raised into a half-smile, but only for a second. "I'm going out for a couple of beers with some friends of mine. Do you want to come?"

"If you say so," I whimpered.

"Come."

*

I got to know his friends in the weeks after that, and I began to rediscover myself. I had never had that kind of companionship before – it made me see things in a different way.

These new friends did not judge me for what I had done badly, or for what I had not yet achieved. The people I used to call friends were only friends while I was successful, but these new friends had no expectations of me, and they included me in their lives without conditions.

These friends became a sounding board for my thoughts and worries, an earthly touchstone for my life rather than having to measure myself against the entire cosmos. I came to value them above all else.

I took a gardening job and started paying Leo some rent. Of course, I had to start making some of my own decisions again, but only small ones. The big decisions, about where my life was going, or how I could inject meaning into it, did not trouble me any more.

Leo became less of a master and more of a mentor for me. I grew to view him very fondly. And what surprised me most was the realisation of how lonely I had been before.

My friends, and Leo – my best friend – have helped me to appreciate the small things in life. The most important things. Now that the burden of aimless ambition has faded away, I can work with them to build a quieter purpose in our lives.

One day I will be dead. People will look back at my life, and they might say I was a martial artist; they might say I was a musician; they might say I was a footballer.

They might even say I was a philosopher, for now that my personality has become less broad and more deep, my thoughts have become deeper too. Recently I have felt the feathers of philosophical inspiration tickling my mind, and it won't be long before it becomes clear enough to commit to paper.

But I think I would prefer it if they said, above all, he was my friend.

First published at www.eastoftheweb.com

A wonderful Italian friend of ours had a badger puppet he named Baggio, after the footballer. He used to bring Baggio when we went out as a group of friends, and he gave it a hilarious puppet-personality. Baggio would boast about how superior he was to the rest of us, having played football for Italy, and written operas, and generally achieved more than us mere mortals could even dream.

In 2006, I was inspired to write a story from Baggio's perspective. How, I wondered, had such a successful and storied individual as Baggio the Badger ended up as the subject of our lowly friend? A literal puppet?

After the story was published, I was delighted that people enjoyed the story even though they didn't know the in-joke: that it was secretly a story about a badger puppet.

Fast forward five years and I discovered, to my amazement, that Abdulla Al Kaabi had adapted Baggio's Story into a short film starring Jean Reno.

I couldn't believe that Jean Reno – The Professional himself! – had played the part of a badger puppet without even knowing.

Fast forward nearly a decade more. Abdulla Al Kaabi commissioned me to write a feature-length screenplay with him. A dream come true, all thanks to Baggio the Badger.

REMISSION

66

Nothing moved for a moment. A clutch had been pressed, my life changed gear.

99

O n an overcast afternoon in late July, hundreds of us stood shoulder to shoulder in the big plaza outside Middlesex Vocational College, waiting for our futures to be decided. The air was thick with humidity and tension, all eyes facing Speaker's Plinth.

"Brown, Camelia: Lunar 4 Geomechanics."

Dean Porter stood atop the plinth wearing a ceremonial gown and a stern expression that made it look like he was delivering a eulogy. As each name and job was read out, there was a ripple somewhere in the crowd. Mostly back-patting and congratulations; sometimes commiserations.

"Dyer, Felix: Lunar 1 Planning."

I stood with Fred, Don and the Olivers (there were two of them), the guys I'd grown closest to while we'd been studying there. We were all hoping to get placed together, on the same mine at least, but it wasn't going to happen. Lunar Corps and the other mining agencies placed grads like us according to academic performance only. No mere social considerations held water.

"Ibsen, Thomas: Lunar 4 Ventilation."

Don had all but flunked out. He'd be bound for maintenance or construction – one of the jobs where you routinely have to shove your head into giant machinery. Fred and one of the Ollies were hoping for the fast track to command. I'd aced my mining modules but embarrassed myself in the space disciplines.

"Idleworth, Frederick: Earthside Launch Mechanic."

Fred jumped up and punched the air, whooping like an American. We put hands on his shoulder, smiled our fakest smiles. Being placed Earthside was even better than command – you could go home each day. I wonder who Freddie's dad had greased up to get him that gig.

The Olivers were up next. Both got placed on Lunar 4. Ollie J got the fast track that he wanted. The logical part of my mind said I should feel happy for him, but I couldn't feel till I heard my name.

"Jackson, Paul: Lunar 2 Engineering."

I'd wanted to go into space ever since I was little. My grandfather used to take me outside past bedtime to point out Venus or Jupiter through the methane miasma that tainted the city sky. He told me to lie in the grass at night next time I went camping and look up – that I wouldn't believe how many stars there were. It was only after he died that I first saw the Milky Way, and then there were so many questions

I wanted to ask him. A question for every star in the sky. But it was too late.

"Judd, Donald: Lunar 4 Construction."

Don's whole body relaxed like a parted vice. He wore a beatific smile. Not because he'd got a crummy job – that was no surprise – but because he was going to Lunar 4 with the two Olivers. I felt sweat pricking my skin as if every pore in my body had dilated. My breathing was fast and choppy, but I couldn't slow it down. Lunar 4. Please, Lunar 4.

The next few names seemed to take a million years. A bubble of blood appeared on my thumb where I was nipping at a hangnail, and then it wouldn't stop bleeding. I sucked the side of my thumb, my consciousness converging until I was aware of nothing but Dean Porter's smug baritone. Then I heard my name.

"Lemont, Archer: Io 1 Generalist."

There was a whooshing sound and time slowed. The sound, I realised, had been a collective intake of breath. Dean Porter was still talking, but everyone seemed to be looking at me. Not just my friends – everyone.

"Well," I said, "talk about your space adventures. Io! I'll have some stories to tell!"

Either they didn't hear me or the words hadn't actually come out. Don put his hand on my shoulder and left it there. The faces of the others were frozen.

"Sorry, Archie," said Don.

"What are you sorry for? I'll be OK."

"I mean . . . the Pit."

"I'll . . . Don't worry. I'll –" My voice cracked. I smiled. Must have looked like something out of Madame Tussauds.

Both Ollies squirmed. Fred crossed his arms and sneered – I couldn't tell if it was discomfort or disapprobation. Don said what needed to be said; something we could all buy into:

"Let's go for a drink."

*

Lucy. Sweet Lucy Pinner. My childhood sweetheart, technically, although we'd both strayed plenty. But we kept ending up back together like a bad habit. Truth is, I'd never slept with another woman without picturing Lucy's limpid blues, although I'd never admit that to her.

So when I stumbled in drunk that night I was glad to see her sitting on my sofa, eating my popcorn and watching old Britcom reruns.

"How'd you get in?" I slurred.

"Gave your landlord sexual favours. He might seem like a meek little Sikh, but he's hung like a hoss."

"I hope he tipped," I said, shucking off my jacket.

"You're pretty drunk. Celebrating, I hope."

"And you're pretty ugly, but I'll be –"

"Sober in the morning? That'll be a first."

I landed next to her, kissed her deeply, then put my arm around her and started firing popcorn into my mouth. "Don't toy with me," I said. "I'm half-cut and emotionally vulnerable."

"I'm just sore I didn't get invited. I don't like being soberer than you – your sway makes me seasick."

"Well, catch up then," I said and reached over to the wine rack. "Red or white?"

"Are we celebrating?"

"No, we're drinking."

"Hm. Make mine a large then. White." She produced a glass from somewhere.

I filled it almost to the brim, kept pouring, then told her, "Say when."

"When!"

"When you want me to stop, of course."

"Stop, stop!" A little wine splashed onto her leg.

"Let me get that," I said. I slunk off the sofa and scooched between her legs, licking the wine from her thigh.

"Huh, you're about as sexy as a pinscher."

"What can I say. I can't resist you."

"You mean I can't be resisted. It's not a weakness of yours, dear, it's my innate charisma. Don't try to fight it."

"Oh I won't."

"But first," she said, grabbing a clump of my hair and gently lifting my head from between her legs, "tell me. Is this a consolation prize? What job did you get?"

"Let's not talk work, let's –"

"Come on, Archie, it can't be that bad. Did they make you a cleaner or something?"

"Not now, I'll tell you tomorrow."

Lucy clamped her legs together. "You'll tell me now."

I gazed up into her eyes and felt the weight of the infinite future. My bones ached with it.

"I'm a Generalist," I said.

"That's . . . good, isn't it? On which base?"

"Io."

Nothing moved for a moment. A clutch had been pressed, my life changed gear. Then, gradually, the wheels engaged again and I continued, headlong.

I settled back on my haunches, kowtowing before Lucy. Her eyes grew wide, and I couldn't look at her any more. I stared at her ruby-painted toenails instead.

Her voice was steady. "How far is Io?"

"Six years. Give or take."

"And how many shuttles are there?"

"Two."

"So six years out, six years there, six years back? Eighteen years?"

"Minimum."

"When do you launch?"

"Ten weeks."

She said nothing for a while. I brushed a fingertip against the almost invisible hairs on her left big toe. She stood and walked out of my line of sight. I refocused onto an old grey carpet stain.

Then I felt her arms reach around me from behind, and her head rest on my shoulder. My heart swelled and my eyes stung. I turned and kissed her; we sank to the floor and lay like that, caressing each other's hair and saying nothing.

I woke the next morning, still on the floor, with aches in muscles I didn't know I had. Lucy wasn't there. I stumbled around tidying up the previous night's debris with a hand over one eye to stop my brain falling out.

Later I went to the bedroom and she was there, sitting on the bed, staring into the middle distance. I sat next to her.

"Sit up straight," I ordered.

She obeyed, correcting her posture.

"Smile," I said.

"I don't want to."

I put my arm around her. She was stiff. "Lucy?"

"Yes?"

"Will you wait for me?"

Her face collapsed as if she'd been punched in the stomach. She shook her head and fat tears rolled down her cheek. "I wish you hadn't asked me that."

"I don't mean wear black and cross your legs for eighteen years. I'm not asking you to be Penelope. I mean . . . I want to marry you and have a family with you and –"

I stopped because she'd thrown her arms around me and started sobbing. It was the first time I'd seen her cry; it was explosive, as if she'd stored up a lifetime of sorrow. I felt no sorrow. Only weight.

*

I'd heard of the Pit, but knew nothing about it. Don filled me in; he always seemed to know more about the obscure space stuff than he did about the basics. Great for trivia, useless for exams.

"P-I-T stands for Preservation for Interplanetary Travel," Don explained, over a pint at the student bar. "Most economical way to send crew to the outer reaches."

"Most economical," I said, "but not the most comfortable, I take it."

"Most practical, anyway. Take the titanium mine on Io. It's mostly automated, just needs a skeleton crew to keep it running – probably less than a dozen people. But it takes six years to get there. So you'd need to bring six years of air, food and water, plus another six years' worth to top up the supply at the Io base, and a further six years' worth for the people you're taking back."

"Six years, six years, six years, I get it," I moaned, leaning my head into my hand and taking a swig of my drink.

"Sorry. Anyway, carrying all those supplies, you'd need a much bigger ship than for an unmanned mission. To keep the miners comfy you need to control atmospheric pressure, carbon dioxide and humidity. You need sleeping areas, exercise facilities, showers . . . And you need more crew – technicians, plumbers –"

"Whores . . ."

Don leaned over the bar and picked up a little salt shaker. He put it on the table between us. "Sputnik 1, the first ever space probe back in the twentieth century, had a payload of 84 kilos. Unmanned. But Sputnik 2 carried a dog. For the sake of keeping that one little puppy alive, you know how much bigger the payload was?"

"How do you know this stuff?"

Don slammed his pint glass next to the salt shaker, splashing some beer onto the table. "509 kilos," he said. "Six times bigger."

Told you Don was crazy on trivia. "I get it. Manned journeys need more room than unmanned, which means less space for titanium, or at least less money for the Space Corps."

"Right. Solution? Don't transport living people."

I stared at him. Downed my drink. "I do *not* like where this is going."

"Instantly you're two-thirds lighter on supplies, you don't need to worry about life-support conditions, you don't need any extra crew, and you don't need to worry about your miners going stir-crazy on the trip."

"Back up. They're going to kill me?"

"The Pit is the future of interplanetary travel. We can send people to stars hundreds of years away. We can –"

"Shut up, Don, and tell me. I'm going to die?"

"Think of it like suspended animation. You get mechanically revived at the other end. Good as new, once you wake up."

"I'll have no pulse, no brain activity, no consciousness . . ."

"Right."

"So I'll be dead."

Don shifted in his seat. "Well, no. At least, not legally."

"Ha!"

"The Pit is actually pretty old technology, but it's only a few years ago that the law got sorted out so the Space Corps could start using it. Routinely, I mean."

"You mean the Pit technicians didn't want to be tried for murder."

"I guess."

"I need another drink."

Don nodded and got up to queue at the bar. I stared at a beer puddle on the table, trying to keep my eyes still, but they were floating on the alcohol in my skull.

Eighteen years. I focused on the thought and tried to feel sad – it seemed appropriate. But I couldn't muster a tear. I tried laughing instead, and that worked pretty well, so that by the time Don came back he found me gaping cross-eyed at the beer puddle, guffawing quietly to myself.

"You OK?" he asked.

"Cheers, buddy." We clinked glasses.

"Look on the bright side."

"There's a bright side?"

"Well, you know – clouds . . . linings . . . When you get back, you'll get two decades' worth of pay at once. And you'll get bumped up to at least Commander."

"Eighteen years to get to Commander? That's not exactly fast."

"But it'll only be six years for you really. In the Pit, you don't even age. Closest you'll ever get to time travel."

"Don't I get some kind of extra compensation for having to do such a long tour? Danger money? Anything?"

Don shrugged his shoulders. Sipped his drink. He seemed lost in thought for a moment, then he looked at me sideways. "How's Lucy?" he said.

*

By mid-August I'd taken to avoiding the student bar altogether. I couldn't stand the constant hangdog looks from everyone as if they felt so sorry for me. They barely knew me.

Besides, it was sunny out. We'd all finished our studies and had jobs starting in a few weeks; meanwhile we had nothing to do. So Fred and I played tennis. Don taught me how to juggle. I joined Don and the Olivers in epic war games with painted miniatures in Ollie J's garden.

And Lucy came round often. We would go out to the patch of grass round the back of my digs, she'd lie with her head in my lap, and we'd talk for hours. We talked about travelling, visiting Thailand or Patagonia, challenging ourselves to get from one city to another on foot, or getting ourselves invited to dinner by the locals. We talked about how many children we wanted – two or three – and how we would bring them up. We talked about what would be the first thing we'd do once I got back.

And twice we dared to make love right there in the sunshine, reckless, heedless of the risk that someone would happen by, spreading ourselves out on the tickling grass and inhaling the primal scent of the soil as if we were making love with the earth itself.

Don and the Olivers shipped out to Lunar 4 in early September; things were pretty quiet after that. I was starting to feel the side effects of the medication I was given to prepare my body for the Pit. Waking up tired, as if I was already half dead, and barely able to coax myself off the sofa all day.

My mum visited a lot during that time, fussing over me relentlessly. She was full of smiles and platitudes. "It'll be fine, Archer. The time will pass before you know it." She made me huge meals that I barely touched for lack of appetite; I told her I felt guilty for not eating what she'd made, but she hugged me and kissed me and said it didn't matter. She told me she was proud of me. It seemed like an odd thing to be proud of.

My sister visited me once, while I was having a check-up in the Corps Medical Centre. I was in bed, wired up to an IV and various monitoring devices. She turned up clutching her handbag with her shoulders hunched, eyes puffy.

"Zel!" I said, grinning. "Great to see you!"

She approached my bedside tentatively, and sat. "You look awful," she said.

"Thank you very much. You don't look so hot yourself."

She reached a finger out and touched the tube protruding from just below my right clavicle, feeling where it entered my skin. "Does it hurt?" she asked.

"They call it a 'port'. All the drugs go in through there. Just before launch they'll give me another port so they can pump all my blood out and replace it with the enriched methanal for the Pit."

"What?"

"Basically embalming fluid. My blood goes into cold storage, and when I land at the other end it gets pumped back into me. Then I get a few electric shocks and boom, I'm back in action. It's a bit more complicated than that, but that's the gist."

Zelda's face stretched – either she'd sat on a pin or she was about to burst into tears. I pretended not to notice and kept talking.

"Here, listen to this," I said, picking up the packet from one of the drugs I'd been taking. "Side effects may include nausea, diarrhoea, fatigue, blah blah blah, oedema and death. Pretty harsh, huh? Mind you, in a sense death is the *desired* effect. Ah, the glamorous life of an astronaut. I –"

She put her hand on mine, held it. I got the message and shut up. Tears were running down her cheeks, but she closed her eyes and composed herself. I offered her a tissue. Then she gave me a fierce look, like she'd taken a huge breath and her whole body was tensed for the release – I dared not move until she spoke.

"I'm pregnant," she said, and suddenly her eyes glittered, her face was soft; she smiled the saddest smile I've ever seen.

My heart swelled. I opened my mouth to congratulate her, and surprised myself by overflowing into tears. Without fully understanding why, I was laughing and sobbing. We were sobbing-laughing together. Without speaking we said a thousand things to each other. With a tilt of her head she told me she'd only just found out, that I was the first to know. With a nod I told her how sorry I was that I wouldn't see her child grow up. With a lopsided smile she told me that she would tell her baby all about me.

My sister and I hadn't always got on. We were always too absorbed in our own lives to look out for each other. But in that moment I saw that she was the best friend I had. I saw how well she knew me, and how much I valued her.

*

The week before launch was a blur. I was on so many different drugs I couldn't trust my senses. I remember seeing my mum; Zelda with her husband; Lucy . . . but I also remember seeing Don, and I can't have seen Don because he was at Lunar 4.

The bed in the Medical Centre became my universe. Nothing existed beyond its boundaries. My left foot hurt and my entire identity became that foot. I had no name, no context, no purpose – my being was reduced to the boiling pain in the fifth metatarsal. Then the pain would subside and I would have a moment of clarity. The hovering face of a nurse would ask me if I was OK and I would smile wanly and nod my head. I would start to say something, but lose the thought.

This cycle of agony and clarity repeated and intensified, woven together with fitful dreams and fevered hallucinations. Images of my mum shouting at my dad for coming home late mixed together with Lucy reading me a spiralling Dylan Thomas poem, and I wasn't sure what was real.

Then gradually, after a million years or half an hour, the moments of clarity became clearer, and the pain duller. I saw beyond my hospital bed and realised I wasn't in the Medical Centre anymore. The room was bigger, plainer. Metal walls. A smell of oil and rotten eggs. A television buzz. Io 1.

A man came by and asked me how I felt. "I'm never drinking again," I said. He asked me again – but then I realised he was asking someone else this time, off to my right. A strange gruff voice responded, "Dead good."

I felt a jarring sense of disorientation. It seemed impossible that I was on some godforsaken rock four million miles from home. Impossible. The room dipped and swayed as I fought a terrible vertigo. I closed my eyes and tried to breathe deeply.

When I opened them again I tried to focus on little things. My throat was dry. I was lying down in a large padded cylinder. The port in my right shoulder was connected to tubes that protruded from the cylinder's white wall. The port in my left thigh was hooked up too. I was as naked and hairless and grey as a newborn mole.

I wiggled my toes, lifted my arm, tried to picture Lucy's face; but I felt an odd sense of detachment, as if I was merely channelling someone else's thoughts. Little aches and pains chased around my body every time I moved as if my veins had grown scales.

The man came back and leaned over me, fiddling with my ports. He was hairless too – his expression was rendered oddly neutral for lack of eyebrows. He moved with a slow grace, as if dancing. My ports were sealed, the tubes disconnected, and he signalled for me to get up.

I sprang up and nearly fell out of the cylinder. My head spun; my fingers clawed for purchase. I hovered in mid-air for a second like a cartoon before falling awkwardly back into the padded Pit. The man – a doctor, I decided – laughed at me.

"One-sixth gravity," he said. "You'll get used to it."

That reeling vertigo again. I clutched the edge of the Pit, white-knuckled, feeling seasick. The doctor moved on to his next patient, leaving me gasping for breath.

"Looking peaky," said the gruff voice.

Through blurred vision I saw that it belonged to a well-built shiny-skinned man sitting up in the Pit next to mine. And beyond him, five more Pits, five more naked Rip van Winkles being awoken from their long slumber.

I nodded, trying not to vomit.

"I'm Masher," he said.

"Masher?" I managed. "That's your name?"

"Naw, but I figure I can be Masher out here. You?"

"I'm –" I retched. A glob of stomach acid burned its way up my throat. I swallowed it back down. "I'm not feeling very well."

"Nice to meet you, Puke-Risk."

*

There were seven of us on Io 1. Five mining generalists, a commander and a doctor. The only life for millions of miles in any direction. The seven crew who had preceded us left the day after we all got out of the Pit – seems they were keen to get home. They'd shown us where everything was and how to run things, but they'd only shown us once, so it took us a couple of weeks to get our heads around everything. Particularly because we all felt like death warmed up. Which, of course, we were.

The seven of us had nicknames for each other. Those who didn't have a nickname ready were given one. Masher, Doc, Two Fish, Lippy, Ghost, Manc . . . I tried to be Shorty, but too late – Puke-Risk had already stuck.

The base was small. There was the loading station, where we'd woken up, two labs, a habitation module with kitchen facilities and beds, a tiny exercise/shower room and an even tinier toilet. There weren't enough rooms for us to be in one each, unless one of us put on a suit and went outside. Anyway, there was a kind of unspoken taboo on being alone for more than a few minutes.

The routine was unbearably monotonous. We worked three shifts, in pairs – the days were about forty-two and a half hours long, which made the shifts just over fourteen hours each. My buddy was usually Masher. The drill buggies and recon drones did the actual work of mining without any human intervention, but we were kept busy with vehicle maintenance, materials processing, geothermal monitoring, tectonic analysis, land surveys, site excursions, shift reports, power-plant duty, and dozens of other things.

In our off-duty time we had to do at least six hours of calisthenics per Io-day, four hours of further study, and usually at least two hours of base safety checks or inventory counts or whatever other mundane make-work Two Fish could come up with. Plus sleeping, twice a day. But even with all that to occupy us, we still ended up with interminable hours of spare time.

We each had a portable tablet that we could sync up to central comms, so we could effectively send and receive emails. But with the vagaries of electromagnetic radiation and random celestial obstructions, it often took several days for a message to get to or from Earth, and sometimes the messages seemed to get lost completely.

When I first synced up my tablet, I had six years' worth of messages from my family and friends. My eyes started stinging when I saw that I had four hundred and thirty-two messages from my mother, and over a hundred and fifty from my sister. I felt a deeper, darker set of emotions when I saw that I had only ten messages from Lucy Pinner.

There were messages too from Don, Fred, both Olivers, a bunch of family friends, and even a few notes from Zelda's son, talking about how in school today he made a castle out of a cardboard box, or how much he didn't like broccoli.

What hurt the most was not that I'd missed six years, but that everybody had got on fine without me. Their lives barrelled on, they didn't miss me or think of me, except as part of an occasional letter-writing exercise, an obligation, a chore. They were getting promoted, married, having children; for me, those milestones were nothing more than half-baked possibilities hovering at the distant edge of a soul-grinding limbo. My life was on pause.

I wrote back to them all. I noticed, though it wasn't my intention, that in all my letters I asked only about them and their lives. I didn't reveal a single thing about myself and my life on Io. Neither did they press me for such details. They asked, but didn't seem to mind when they got no answer.

The messages seemed to reinforce the distance between us rather than shrink it. So, as time went on, I wrote less. Except to Lucy. To her, I wrote every day. Personal things. Deep meandering desperate thoughts that I'd never have admitted to her directly. Her scarce replies were blandly encouraging, as if she were hedging her bets. She spoke of the various false starts in her acting career; of drudge bar work to pay the bills; of the people in her life; of men she met and discarded. She said she loved me. I read every word she wrote a thousand times.

*

"Race you back," said Masher over the helmet radio.

"No way. I'm not giving Two Fish an excuse to put me on cleaning duty again," I responded.

"Two Fish is a prick," said Masher. "Screw him."

"He can hear us, you know."

"Yah, like he'd bother to listen. Switch to fifteen."

I rolled my eyes. Masher and I were riding a couple of recon drones on manual override, having done a sampling run on the beta seam. The Jupiter rise was in full flood ahead of us, its marbled surface of dusty orange dominating the horizon. The sun looked like a dull penny at our backs. I switched frequency.

". . . read me? Can you read me?" Masher's voice crackled.

"I'm not going to race."

"Listen, Puke-Risk, Two Fish has got too big for his boots. You know it, I know it. So we're gonna stage a mutiny."

I sighed. "How would you run the base any different?"

"Manc is well up for it. Lippy'll bend. Doc doesn't count, and Ghost is a pussy. No more base safety checks two hours after we finished the last one. No more yes sir no sir. And we could all stop taking those bloody pills and grow back some hair."

"You've been talking about this for days."

"But now's the time. By my reckoning, tomorrow it's an Earth year since we got here. It'd be symbolic. A changing of the guard."

We parked the drones and switched them back to auto, then bounce-walked to the pressure lock. We talked procedure while the air and psi normalised, but the temperature always took longer. It had to heat up from minus 150 C.

"We've really only been here one year?" I said.

"Time crawls when you're having none," said Masher, looking at me through his helmet glass. The pressure lock was too cramped for personal space; I could see the red veins in his eyes.

"Mash, do you get the fear sometimes that this'll never end?"

"What d'you mean?"

"I mean like we're in some kind of infinite loop on this rock. Like we can get to the end of a day, but as soon as we wake up we're back at the start again? Maybe we really died, and this is some kind of Sisyphean punishment."

"Sissy what?"

I squinted to read the analogue temperature gauge. "Two zero four Kelvin and climbing."

Masher verified my reading with his digital gauge. "Check. I'm counting the days, buddy. Every sleep is one closer to going home."

My eyes focused on the ghostly reflection of my face in Masher's helmet glass. "But what's home?

It's a memory. Doesn't exist any more," I mused. Not that Masher was paying attention. "D'you ever think, 'Why me?'"

"Naw. Why *not* me? I can take it better than most, I reckon."

"Two niner zero Kelvin and stable. Safe temperature achieved."

"Check."

We went through all the checks once more – that's how we survived in space, double- and triple-checking everything – and let ourselves into the base. We took off our heavy suits and skipped to the habitation module. Two Fish was at the mess table playing cards with Doc.

"Sampling excursion complete, sir," I said.

"Heya, Puke-Risk," he responded. "Masher."

Masher pointedly ignored the greeting and sidled to the kitchenette to make a hot drink (actually a tepid drink – the boiling point of water was lukewarm).

Two Fish shook his head wearily. "Masher, you're on cooking detail today. Puke-Risk, you're auditing the titanium in the shipping bay. Make sure the ore is packed in as tightly as possible."

"Yes, sir."

"Soon as the two of you have done your shift report we'll take over."

"Who's on shift with you?" I asked.

Two Fish responded by looking in the direction of the lav. He looked concerned.

Doc picked up on his expression and said, "Ghost has been a while in there, eh?"

Two Fish put down his cards, got up and walked over to the toilet. Masher and I exchanged glances, then watched him as he yanked the door open. We couldn't see what he saw; his bulky back blocked the view.

"Need some help here!" he shouted, and dropped to his knees. He took his vest off, revealing his giant tattoo of two fish swirling together into a yin-yang.

The three of us – Masher, Doc and I – rushed over. At first I didn't realise what I was seeing. Everything was slick wet, Ghost was on the floor and Two Fish was wrapping his vest around Ghost's shoulder. A metallic tang in the air. Tackiness underfoot. The vest blushed crimson where it touched Ghost's pale skin.

Blood. Everywhere, blood.

Two Fish bent over to start CPR, but Doc stopped him. "He's pulled out his port," said Doc. "He's dead."

Doc and Two Fish exchanged a glance. Two Fish nodded, then barked orders. "We need to get him to the Pit as soon as possible. Our only chance."

Two Fish, Masher and I picked up Ghost's body. Doc ran out of the habitation module and we followed him. I tried not to think of how painful it must have been to pull out his port. Had he been so unhappy? I'd known the man for a year, yet we'd only ever spoken in small circles. I knew so little of him.

I felt unnaturally aware of the port in my own chest, just below my right shoulder, like a splinter. I felt light-headed.

"Puke-Risk!" shouted Masher. "Pull yourself together!"

But it was too late. I dropped to the floor and vomited my guts out.

*

Ghost lay in one of the Pits, grey as winter clouds. He was conscious now, but something behind his eyes had stayed dead.

Once Doc had replaced Ghost's port, the Pit had done its job: drained the rest of his blood away and preserved his body for a while, then slowly fed his blood back in. Brought him back from beyond the veil. He spoke occasionally, to request water or pain relief. He moved when instructed to for his physiotherapy. But he didn't seem whole any more.

I sat next to him, reading him one of the classic novels that had been preloaded onto my tablet. *Twenty Thousand Leagues Under the Sea*. I knew the others thought I was weird for spending time with him, but they left me alone. The whole base had been pretty subdued since Ghost tried to kill himself. Masher's energy for mutiny had certainly vanished.

I found that I'd stopped reading. I'd been staring at the page, but couldn't focus. Ghost was staring at the ceiling, oblivious. My mind kept plummeting back to Lucy Pinner's last letter.

I'd received it three days before. In it she spoke of the play she'd been writing, her insomnia, a pending audition for a TV ad, the unsanitary toilet habits of her flatmate's cat; and, right at the end, a passing mention that she and Don had been seeing each other for the last few months.

She'd written before of having been on dates, of relationships that had fizzled out before they'd really started – that hadn't bothered me. But sleeping with my best friend? Whenever I thought about it my stomach hurt so much I couldn't speak.

Doc walked in, hesitating at the doorway when he saw me. "Mind if I . . .?" he said, pointing at Ghost.

I nodded.

He adjusted a dial on the Pit that controlled Ghost's sedation level. Ghost closed his eyes and became even less responsive than usual. Doc sat next to the Pit and set about replacing the bandages on Ghost's port.

"You've been a bit preoccupied lately," said Doc.

I didn't respond.

"Ghost'll be all right," Doc said, consoling. "If that's what's bugging you."

Again, a silence stretched between us. I tried to find words. "I . . . He . . . I mean . . . Why don't you let him die?"

Doc's face fell into a humourless frown. "It's not his decision to make."

"Up here, we've got nothing," I stammered. "It's the only thing we can choose any more."

"The safety and function of the base rely on a full complement of crew. You signed up to this deal when you came aboard. You are not permitted to die."

"Haven't you got any sense of mercy?" I said, blinking back a tear. "Damn your Hippocratic Oath. The only way to help this man is to let him make his own choice."

Doc's face softened. Pity? Woe? I couldn't tell. "Think of his future," he said. "Think of his family and friends."

"They would tell you to let him die too."

"They would at least want to say goodbye. They have the right."

"We're basically dead already. This is no life. We put so much effort into clinging on, and for what? So we can go through the same tiny hell for another day. For another thousand days."

Doc looked down. Said nothing.

I sighed deeply, feeling suddenly angry that my eyes had watered up. I wanted to smash my tablet on the floor and stomp into the pressure lock without my suit on. But the feeling dissipated, leaving my heart heavy, as if a piece of my soul had evaporated. "Sorry," I said, my voice cracking. "It's not your fault."

Doc gave me an infinitely gentle look, like he wanted to enfold me in his arms and let me sob my problems away. But something held him back. A veneer of professionalism? Misplaced machismo? His own fear of falling apart?

He'd always seemed so confident, as if this terribly claustrophobic existence held no discomfort for him, as if he was in his element. But for a split second I saw past the mask. I saw a frightened child. I saw myself.

*

It felt unreal when we got news that the shuttle was arriving. Six Earth years had passed, and it was finally time to go home. There was a frenzy of activity to unload the supplies, load up the titanium, prepare for the Pit, revive the new crew. I've never been happier to see a corpse!

By then the seven of us were old hands; bound together by shared scars. Older than before. Masters of our tiny realm. We cultivated a carnival atmosphere, collectively suppressing the nerves that niggled at the back of our minds. Going home was to be celebrated, purely; voicing any doubt was taboo. Even Ghost managed a tiny smile.

We showed the befuddled new crew around. I felt bad for them; I wanted to warn them how hard it would be, but there were no words, so I settled for upbeat platitudes. And then it was time for us to enter the Pit. We had done all the material preparation, but suddenly I panicked that I was mentally far from ready.

But the sickness took over, and it was done.

I woke up bleary-eyed, saw that I was in the Corps Medical Centre back on Earth. I felt the same jarring vertigo as my brain denied with all its might that six more years and four million miles had passed.

An old woman kissed me on the cheek. I looked at her, confused. She stood back – my mother was standing next to her, with a strange man wearing an even stranger fashion of jeans and U-neck shirt. But she couldn't be my mother, she was too young.

No; she was my sister. Zelda. And the man standing next to her – her son. My nephew. So the old lady was . . .

"Mum!" I cried, and tears filled my eyes, falling in rivulets to my temples.

The four of us wept or fidgeted or tried to smile, but none of us found a word to say. Finally, my mum broke the silence. She leaned over, navigating around the tubes that protruded from my body, and gave me an awkward hug. "Welcome home, Archer."

Archer. My name was Archer. And I was home. I smiled more widely than I had done for years.

I got out of there as soon as I could, and I was on a high for days. I stayed with my mother, spending each day just walking around the city. I revelled in feeling healthy, safe. The sun felt like a caress. I felt drunk on the smells of grass, and exhaust fumes, and hot bread, and summer air – the noise of life was like music. For twenty minutes I stood in the park, enthralled by the innocent energy of a pet puppy. I sat in a café and took two hours to finish one cup of coffee.

A week passed, my hair started growing back a little, and my mum suggested I get in touch with my old friends. I realised I had been trying not to think of them, as if meeting them again would spoil the memory of how we were before. But once I decided it was time, my nerves sublimated into excitement. I told myself it wouldn't be like old times, but it would be all right.

"I want to see Lucy," I said.

My mum's lips tightened and she asked me to sit down. "I didn't tell you before, because . . ." She hesitated. Cleared her throat. "Four years ago, while you were travelling, Lucy and Don got married."

I nodded. Looked at the floor.

"I'm sorry, sweetie."

"No, it's – OK," I said. My mind was a swirl of emotions, but a sharp beam of light cut through the fog and convinced me that it really was OK.

*

I rang the bell, took a long, deep breath. The door opened, and there stood Lucy Pinner, looking about twelve months pregnant. When she saw me, her jaw hit the floor. "Archie."

"Lucy," I said. "You look . . . old."

She stared at me a moment like she'd been slapped in the face. Then she laughed, and the years fell away. She waddled down onto the porch, put her arms around me and gave me a deeply inappropriate kiss. I felt stirred in ways I'd forgotten I could.

"You always knew how to charm the ladies," she said, smiling broadly.

"Hey, you had it coming."

"I have been a very bad girl."

"I forgive you. Let's kiss again before your husband gets here."

"Oh, you cad."

"What can I say. I can't resist you."

"You mean, I can't be resisted." She half smiled, her head tilted, her cobalt eyes looking deep into mine. She kept her arms locked around me, the bump of her tummy pressing against my stomach. Her brow creased. "I know you're the one who had to go away, but you don't know how difficult it's been."

I nodded, held my palm to her cheek.

"I waited," she said. "Tried to wait. But I convinced myself . . . I thought you'd never come back. Don was an absolute gentleman. I was a wreck – he looked after me for years."

"Are you happy?" I said.

Her expression was impossible to read. She held up a finger, pressed it gently against my lips. "You'd better come inside."

I followed her in. She led me through the hall into the lounge. I sat on the edge of a pleasantly worn sofa. She gave me a compact smile, then walked out of the room. As I waited for her to return my eyes scanned the bookshelves. Biographies of famous actresses were mixed in with mining textbooks. There was a row of framed pictures of Lucy and Don together. He'd gained a few pounds and wrinkles, his hair was silvering, but he looked happy. They looked happy together. My stomach churned.

At the end of the row was a picture of me.

I heard Lucy padding back into the room behind me. I turned to her, smiling, and my smile froze. She stood before me, glowing with soft energy, wearing not a stitch. I knew as soon as I saw her that this image would burn itself into my mind for the rest of my life.

"Don . . .?" I said

"He's away." Her smile was like a cat's. I let my eyes explore her, savouring the moment. She glided to the sofa and lay across it, resting her head on my lap. I was tense, at first, but eventually I relaxed, letting myself melt into the sofa cushions.

"I can't believe you're back," she said.

"I can't believe you're pregnant."

She laughed. I stroked her hair and we sat there together, saying nothing for a while.

"How long before they call you up for another tour?" she asked.

"Dunno. Could be weeks, could be years. My experience'll probably qualify me for another ridiculously distant assignment."

"Don't go."

"At least life up there is pretty simple."

"Don't go."

"I wish I had the choice."

She didn't say anything after that, and neither did I, until the sun went down. At some point she'd fallen asleep. I stood up as slowly as I could, covered her with a blanket, and left.

As I sat on the train I thought about my future. I had money, and freedom, for now; I was healthy. Maybe I'd go away somewhere. Maybe the best gift I could give to Lucy and Don would be to leave them alone. Or maybe it was for my sake. The longer I thought, the less I knew.

When I got home to my mother's house, I saw a letter from the Space Corps waiting for me on the dining table. I went to bed, leaving it unopened.

First published in Bleed (Perpetual Motion Machine Publishing, 2013)

In 2013, I was asked to contribute a story for a cancer-themed horror anthology called Bleed, *published to raise money for* The National Children's Cancer Society. Bleed *turned out to be brilliant, among the highest standard of writing of any anthology I've been published in, but at first I thought it was a terrible idea: Can you imagine anything more depressing than reading a whole book of stories monstrously personifying cancer? I only wanted to contribute a story if I could come up with an angle no-one else would be exploring.*

So I wrote Remission. *It's a science fiction space tale, but also a metaphor for the less obvious side effects of dealing with a serious illness: loneliness, loss, fear, isolation, stress on family and friends. My newborn baby daughter was severely ill when I wrote it, and the story is infused with some of the trauma and desperate hopefulness I was feeling. (Thankfully, she recovered!)*

RESOURCES FOR TEACHERS: DEATH BY SCRABBLE

Comprehension questions

- Why is the main character upset?
- What happens when the main character plays the word ZAPS?
- Why does the wife ask the main character if he is cheating?
- What happens to the main character at the end of the story?

Inference questions

- Who is the protagonist? Who is the antagonist?
- Why does the main character hate his wife?
- What kind of person is the main character? What is your evidence to support this?
- Does your opinion of the wife change at the end of the story? Why or why not?

Point of view questions

- Who is the narrator of the story?
- From what point of view is the story told?
- How might the story be different if told from the other character's point of view?

Structure questions

- What do we learn during the introduction/ exposition?

- How does the first word, JINXED, set the whole story in motion?
- How does the author build tension during the rising action?
- What is the climax of the story?

Further questions
- What detail foreshadows the end of the story?
- How does the atmosphere enhance the story?
- Did the main character deserve his fate? Why or why not?
- What does the author want the reader to learn from the main character's fate? (In other words, what is the theme?)

Exercises
- Identify at least two conflicts in the story.
- Identify how the story uses both situational and dramatic irony.
- Use your imagination, and write a paragraph sharing the wife's thoughts (her point of view) during the last part of the story.

Examples of figurative language
- Onomatopoeia
    * "I can hear buzzing insects outside."
    * "Clack clack. Clack clack."
- Personification
    * "The heat of the sun is pushing at me through the window."
- Hyperbole
    * "I don't think I've spoken to anyone except

my wife since Thursday morning."

* "If she wasn't around, I'd be doing something interesting right now. I'd be climbing Mount Kilimanjaro. I'd be starring in the latest Hollywood blockbuster."

- Metaphor
    * "I feel a terrible rage build up inside me. Some inner poison slowly spreading through my limbs."

MORE FROM CHARLIE FISH

Charlie Fish is a popular short-story writer and screenwriter. His stories have been published in several countries and inspired dozens of short film adaptations. Since July 1996, he has edited www.fictionontheweb. co.uk, the longest-running short-story site on the web. He was born in Mount Kisco, New York in 1980; and now lives in south London with his wife and daughters.

Fiction on the Web is a huge collection of brilliant stories from authors around the world. Enjoy reading the stories online, rate and comment, or submit your own at www.fictionontheweb.co.uk.

- Funny stories – for when you need a laugh
- Creepy stories – to make your hair stand on end
- Fantastic stories – orcs, swords, magic and fantasy
- Futuristic stories – many worlds of science fiction
- Criminal stories – crooks and detectives
- Real-life stories – everyday life and relationships

FINDING CHARLIE FISH ONLINE

Website: www.fictionontheweb.co.uk

Email: charlie@fictionontheweb.co.uk

Twitter: @fishcharlie

THE BEST OF FICTION ON THE WEB

Volume 1: 1996-2017

Foreword by Julia Bell

Featuring stories by Rob Boffard, Rotimi Babatunde, Hanja Kochansky, Fred Skolnik, Anne Goodwin and 49 other authors.

Edited by Charlie Fish

THE BEST OF FICTION ON THE WEB

To celebrate Fiction on the Web's 21st birthday, a charitable collection was published featuring 54 of the best stories that have ever appeared on the site.

All proceeds from the sale of this book are donated to the Guy's and St Thomas' NHS Foundation Trust. This is possible thanks to Fiction on the Web's loyal patrons, whose contributions paid for the copy-editing, design and typesetting of the book.

You can buy the book from Amazon.

"54 irresistible short stories. Buy 'em without a blink."

– Richard E. Grant

Extract from the book's introduction:

The fifty-four stories collected here represent the diversity of the stories I publish at Fiction on the Web. The first story, "Above Candles", was the fifth I ever published, way back in 1996; over two decades later, when choosing the stories for this volume, I still vividly remembered the opening paragraphs in which a priest gives a penance to a young orphan for killing two hundred and twenty-seven men. (Three Hail Marys does the trick.)

Nine other stories made the cut from the olden days of Fiction on the Web, before I gave the site a major facelift. The rest are from the last five years. These stories lingered in my brain because they made me laugh out loud ("CLAM$", "Smart Car"), or openly sob in the middle of the staff canteen ("One Oh for Tillie", "What the Creek Carries Away"). Some evoked a sense of wonder ("The Bird on Silver Strand", "The Rooming House"), and some a visceral fear ("East", "War Baby").

These stories have transported me all over America — Alaska to Maine; Baltimore to Los Angeles — and the UK — Belfast to Scarborough; Glenlivet to London. Further afield as well: Canada, France, Nigeria, the Philippines, New Zealand. (The one set in the Philippines, "Gladiator", is about jungle children betting on spider battles.)

Let's not forget the crisply realised fantasy worlds, full of hardship and redemption ("Across the Oar", "The Place of Endurance"). And the magical tales that take place in a world that's almost ours, but with longer necks ("The Neck"), less solid walls ("The Wall"), or revenant relatives ("Relativity").

The themes of the stories cover huge swathes of the human experience. Love and betrayal ("Hearts and Darts", "The Kindness of Strangers"); justice and redemption ("One on One", "The Right of Wrong"); life and death ("Lost in Glass Slippers", "The Bridge"); sex with space aliens ("Purr", "Spurs that Jingle Jangle Jingle").

The stories are categorised according to the six genres I use at Fiction on the Web. But even within each category, several genres are explored. The "criminal" stories here include a heist, a noir, a caper, a courtroom drama, a corporate conspiracy, and a sweeping condemnation of corruption in the upper echelons of the Catholic Church. (The latter is "Vatican Bag Man".)

Some of my favourite authors are here: "The Debacle" by Beryl Ensor-Smith is one of twenty-five delightful comedies of hers I've published, about gossiping wives in small-town South Africa. I can't get enough of Hanja Kochansky's wonderful autobiographical anecdotes, as in "Goodbye Butterfly". And some authors have gone on to great things after featuring in Fiction on the Web: Rob Boffard has published a series of breathtaking science fiction novels. Rotimi Babatunde won the Caine Prize for African Writing, and has written plays staged in several theatres including London's Young Vic.

Printed in Poland
by Amazon Fulfillment
Poland Sp. z o.o., Wrocław

90481631R00171